House of Women

House of Women

Lynn Freed

Flamingo
An Imprint of HarperCollins*Publishers*

Flamingo
An imprint of HarperCollins *Publishers*
77–85 Fulham Palace Road,
Hammersmith, London W6 8JB

Flamingo is a registered trade mark of
HarperCollins *Publishers* Limited

www.**fire**and**water**.com

Published by Flamingo 2002
1 3 5 7 9 8 6 4 2

First published in the USA by Little, Brown and Company, 2002

This novel is entirely a work of fiction.
The names, characters and incidents portrayed in it are
the work of the author's imagination. Any resemblance to
actual persons, living or dead, events or localities is
entirely coincidental.

Set in Galliard

A catalogue record for this book
is available from the British Library

ISBN 0 00 713329 4

Printed and bound in Great Britain by
Clays Ltd, St Ives plc

For Jess

Acknowledgments

For the gift of time, peace, and a beautiful place in which to write, I thank the Corporation of Yaddo, the Bellagio Study and Conference Center, and the Bogliasco Foundation. Judy Clain's enthusiasm and wise counsel have seen me through. And to Jennifer Rudolph Walsh — whirlwind of intelligence and energy — I owe this book. Thank you.

Part One

❦ 1 ❦

The Syrian stands on the terrace, staring down into the bay. His head and shoulders are caught in the last of the light, massive, like a centaur's. He could be Apollo on his chariot with his hair blown back like that. Or Poseidon. Or Prometheus. He is the darkest white man I have ever seen. It is a sort of gilded darkness, gleaming and beautiful. Even an old man can look like a god, I think.

But, of course, he isn't old. He is just older than I am, much older. I am seventeen and a half and have just lost twelve pounds at the slimming salon. My body is curved and firm and brown. Until now, I have been plain, as my mother is plain, but in a different way. My mother is slim and elegant and plain. I have been sallow and lumpy and awkward, and too clever by half, as she says.

Since I lost weight, she has become more watchful than ever. If a boy whistles at me on the street, she says he is common rubbish, he wants one thing and one thing only, and if I give in, I will be his forever. The result is that every night I dream of common rubbish. Common rubbish comes to watch me sleeping, to adore me as I sleep. When we go out in the car, I am always on the lookout for common rubbish. And yet, walking on the street, I dread their attention. They are callow and leering, and I am full of phrases of contempt.

The Syrian turns. He shades his eyes against the sun and smiles. "Join me?" he says, holding up his whiskey and soda.

I rub at something on my foot, looking away to hide the flush in my cheeks and neck and ears. If my mother were to see me like this, she would throw him out and cancel the dinner. When my father phoned to ask whether his Syrian friend might come, she did not slam down the phone as she usually does. She hung out her blue silk dress and told Maude to make *vol au vent* and *crème caramel*. She likes to surprise my father like this, the way he once surprised her, walking into her dressing room one night and taking her into his arms without even asking.

My father has never lived with us. He has never lived with my mother, either. He lives with one of his other women, or at his house inland, or on his motor launch, tied up at the Esplanade. He is large like the Syrian, and rich, and he is used to getting what he wants. But with my mother, he gets only as far as the dining room table. And sometimes into the lounge afterwards for coffee. When he comes for dinner, it is I who ask Maude to stew guavas for him, and to make a custard to go with it. I am the one who remembers that he takes two lumps of Demerara in a demitasse of black coffee.

I am not his first child, nor, I suppose, will I be the last. But I am the one he has always wanted for himself. Perhaps this is because he cannot have me. Or because my cleverness makes him laugh, as my mother's must once have done. When he laughs at me, she makes a show of flapping out the tablecloth she is embroidering for my trousseau, asking which colour for the basket, which for the stems? She knows that the idea of a marriage will infuriate him. And she is right. "I bloody well hope you're not going to be pulled into *that* stinking swamp," he shouts at me.

My mother herself has never wanted to be in that stinking swamp. She is an opera singer. If it weren't for Hitler, she might have been world famous. But she had to leave the Conservatoire, where she was studying, and hide away. And then, near the end of the War, she was found out and sent to the camps like everyone else, high and low. After it was over, she got on a ship as soon as she could and came here, to the bottom of Africa, where you can be the greatest lyric soprano on earth and no one in the real world would ever even know.

Every week, she drives inland to see Katzenbogen, her psychoanalyst, who also survived the camps. They speak the same language, she says. More than this, the world is mad, and you need to know how to live in it. It takes half a day to get to him, and half a day to get back. And she is always coming home with new ideas.

Last week, she put down her grip in the hall and said, "Compared to the War, what was your father?"

I know enough never to answer such questions. Long before I was born, she found out about my father's other women, and she has hated him with all her fury ever since.

"Compared to the War, what was your father?" she roared at me again. "An accident of Fate! A nonentity! A joke!"

After that, it was as if the War itself had become her real lover, had been her real lover right from the beginning. It is a cruel lover, a deadly lover, there in every shadow like a spider, a snake. And I am jealous of it.

The Syrian walks up from the terrace, onto the verandah. "Windy out there," he says.

I nod. He has a scarf tied at his neck, like a film star. When he looks at me, all my cleverness vanishes, all my phrases of contempt.

"That is my ship down there," he says, leaning against the other pillar.

I look, but I am thinking only of the *broderie anglaise* that I am to wear tonight. It is ridiculously childish with its laced bodice and puffed sleeves.

"I brought some presents for you," he says, pointing to the table. "For your mother and for you both."

I have seen them there, four boxes with beautiful bows and wrappings. When my father brings me presents, I am never to open them until he has left. "Money is as money does," my mother says, holding up a scarf, or a jewelry box, or a book. And then she goes through to the kitchen to give the present to Maude.

My father will be late tonight. He is always late. And always my mother and I wait upstairs until he has been shown into the lounge and made to wait himself. She likes to see him look up as we walk in together. Time after time, he is to regret what he cannot have for himself, what he cannot buy for all the money in the world.

But this time, it is I who have waited. All afternoon I have sat behind the curtains of the sleeping porch, hoping that my father's friend would arrive early. Except for my father, and Dr. Slatkin, and Braughton, the conductor of the civic orchestra, no white man has ever come into our house before. "Let them wait at the gate," my mother likes to say. "Let them die of waiting."

Tomorrow she leaves for her trip inland. Already she is shouting down to the servants. Every week, they are called into the hall and told that Maude will be taking over the household for the days that she is gone, that Maude and only Maude will be in charge of me. This she says in case my father thinks of bribing the gardener or the housegirl to open the gate and let him in.

It has always been this way. When the girls at the convent asked why I could never come to their parties, I told them we had a cottage in the mountains to which we went every weekend — my father, my mother, and I. They didn't believe me, of course. They knew who my mother was, everyone knew. They saw her huddled with the nuns, and Maude waiting at the gate to take me home every Friday afternoon. They must have seen the padlock on our gate when they drove past. But whatever they knew, I lived with my secret as if it, too, were a lover. Every Friday night, I handed my diary to my mother, and then lay with my head in her lap as she read what I had written. "Fat?" she would cry, lifting the notebook to look down at me. "Who says that you are fat?"

"It is winter where I live," the Syrian says.

"In Syria?"

He smiles. "Oh no," he says, "not there." And then suddenly he reaches out and closes his hand around my foot. "Do you know what a beautiful woman you are?"

I know that I am not a woman, I am a girl, and that I have a sharp nose like my father, a sharp tongue to go with it. My mother has often told me this. But with his hand on my foot I forget about my mother, absolutely forget her. I forget the Syrian too, the way he was separated from me down there on the terrace. Up here we are invisible in the silence, he and I. We are his hand on my foot. It is a beautiful hand, with beautiful long fingers.

"Forgive me," he says, sitting back. He folds his arms and looks out again at his ship.

I draw my legs in, hold them by the ankles as if I want to keep them from him. But I don't. I want him to reach over again and take them in his hands and tell me everything about myself. I would believe him, anything he said. When his car drew up at last, and I saw him climb out and shade his eyes to look up at the house, right up at the windows of the sleeping porch where I was sitting, it was as if I had been waiting for him always, all my life. Even as I slipped out of my sandals and crept down the back stairs, stopping at the bottom until Maude had delivered the drinks tray to him — even as I ran along the pantry passage and through the dining room, out onto the verandah, I knew that nothing they could do would stop me now. Not even if they caught me. Not even if they dug their nails into my flesh and screamed for the police.

"I sail tomorrow," he says.

I can hear my mother in her dressing room. She is humming, she is happy. "I've never seen snow," I say, standing up, "I've never even needed a coat."

When I come upstairs, my mother is at her dressing table, smiling as she pats on her rouge. I know her body better than my own, naked and clothed, front, back, sitting, standing. Her flesh is pale as dough, innocent by contrast to mine. I love to watch her roll off her corset, loosen her enormous breasts from her bra. A girl at school taught her how to strap them down when they began to grow, she says, and that is why they hang down the way they do. It is always someone else's fault.

I stand behind her and hug her tight. She has her afternoon smell, a little sour, and I breathe it in. She reaches up and holds my arms, runs her nails lightly over my skin. "Shouldn't you be getting dressed, darling?" she says. "One nonentity is here already. And I think I hear the other one now."

She always hears my father long before he rings the bell, even before the dogs roar up to the front door, jumping and wagging. It is as if she is half animal herself, hiding in the long grass, waiting for the right moment to pounce.

I don't ask her why she has allowed the Syrian into our house. If I did, she could suddenly cancel the dinner and refuse to go down at all. Perhaps she has invited him so that he may fall in love with her under the eyes of my father — so that, once again, my father will know that he is not the only man on this earth. She has laid out her best black evening pearls and her pearl-and-diamond clips. When she makes up her mind, men forget that she is not a beauty and fall madly in love with her.

I watch her pull on her black corset and then her silk stockings, taking great care with the seams. "Hadn't you better get dressed?" she says, taking her diamond watch out of its box. "Help me with the zip, will you, darling? Thanks."

She opens both wardrobe doors to look at herself in the mirrors, front and back. She is shining in the blue silk dress, black-haired and shining. She is Salome, she is Delilah, she is Mary Magdalene. It is impossible now that the Syrian's hand was on my foot, impossible that I listened when he told me I was beautiful. Who am I?, I wonder, staring over her shoulder.

Who am I?, breathing her in, drunk already on her Madame Rochas.

"I'm going down without you," she says, checking herself in the mirror one last time. I hang over the banister to watch her descend as if she were going a great distance, leaving me behind. "Ma," I say, "I'm going to wear my green velvet." But she is already in the hall, at the door of the lounge.

"Ah!" she cries, looping her voice around the Syrian, around my father, too. "Thea will be down in a minute. Or in an hour. Or not at all."

When I do come down, she says nothing about the green velvet, or my flaming cheeks and ears. She makes room for me next to her on the couch as usual. But I slump into the rocking chair instead, and set it going.

"Stop it!" she says, "you're making me seasick."

My father comes over and offers me his hand. He lifts me from the chair and leads me to his friend. "This is my Theadora," he says, "my jewel, my diadem."

I know that they are playing a game, my father and his friend, a game whose aim is to leave my mother out. I turn to her. Her arms and her neck are creamy in the lamplight, but her face is pale, almost white, and her cheekbones are livid with rouge. "I'm going to tell the kitchen that we're coming in," she says.

I wish now that I had worn my *broderie anglaise,* and sat next to her on the couch, and never, never gone out onto the verandah this afternoon. I might as well have stabbed her in the heart, or pushed her head underwater and held it down.

"This one has opinions on every bloody thing under the sun," my father says, still holding on to my shoulder.

"My opinion is that it would be nice if you would dress for

dinner once in a while," I say. I have never spoken to him as my mother does, I have never dared to. When I am cheeky to him, I mean it to be charming. But now his khaki shorts and brown knees and cocky smile make me want to punish him. I don't care if he finds another favourite. I don't care.

He slaps the Syrian on the shoulder. "See?" he cries. "See?"

My mother opens the French doors into the dining room. The table is laid with the best cloth and the good silver. There are wine glasses out, and candles lit. *"Entrez!"* she says.

She sits at the top of the table, watching the men with suspicion. She knows now that inviting the Syrian has backfired, that nothing she can do will wipe the smile off my father's face. He raises his glass to her and says, "Navy becomes you, my dear."

"Pouf!" she says, waving him away with her hand. "It's midnight blue."

The evening is lost, but still she struggles. "Do you have children?" she asks the Syrian, laying a hand on my shoulder.

He shakes his head. He has a villa, he says, and a garden, and two beautiful Irish setters.

"Ah!" she says, "that's a shame."

I want to save her, but I don't know how. I am desperate to save her, to catch him up somehow. "Why are you going back by ship?" I ask.

My father cocks his head and turns to his friend. "Yes, monsieur, why exactly are you taking a ship?"

The Syrian smiles. "Because," he says, "I am terrified of flying."

I know this to be another joke, I can see from the look on my father's face. So can my mother. "Are your people prone to taking sea voyages?" she asks.

Ah, he says, sitting back, the real reason is that he loves the sea, and he loves ships. They cover the real distance in time and space. These days, people are always in a rush. They cannot wait to get there, and then they cannot wait to leave again.

All this he says to my mother. But then, when she gets up to serve the pudding, he turns to me at last. He stares at me the way he stared down at his ship on the bay. If I were not seventeen and a half, I would be able to see his sadness, and his longing, and his hope. I would also see my father's cold eyes watching. But my ears, my neck, my thighs have caught fire all at once. My throat is closing up and I need to swallow. I need to stand and help my mother serve too, but I don't. I take a drink of wine and look back at him, free and easy. I am Delilah myself, I am the lowest of the low, but I cannot help it. I want him to find me beautiful again. I want to be twenty-one, and free to look wherever I like.

When she comes to sit on my bed that night, she feels my forehead. "What's the matter?" she says. "Do you want me to put off tomorrow's trip?"

Never has she made such a suggestion. As a child, I used to beg her not to go inland to Katzenbogen. I would cling to her neck and cry for her to stay. Once, when I had measles, she did stay, but with such bad temper that I never begged again. Now, thinking she might actually stay, I am wild for her to go. I hold out my arms and she bends to me, careful of her hair. "I want you to stay with me," I say. "Please."

She sits back up. "I think the dinner has upset us both," she says. "A great mistake."

"The Ring of the Nonentities."

She does not scold me for this, she even lets out one of her laughs. "That so-called friend of your father's probably had a wife and murdered her," she says. "They kill them for their jewelry, you know, burn down the so-called villa with the wife locked in it. Quite barbaric!"

"Oh, Ma!" I say. Tears begin to roll into my hair, into my ears. "You've got the wrong country for a change."

She feels my forehead again. "If you need me," she says, "you know where I'll be." She always says this when she is going inland. But only Maude knows where she is. And if I ask Maude for the phone number, she says, "Curiosity killed the cat."

Maude is a Roman Catholic, and her room is next to mine. Every night, she lights a candle to the Virgin Mary, which she won't blow out, even though my mother has ordered her to do so. She puts on her hairnet and kneels before her dressing table, where she has arranged a crocheted doily, and the candle, and a statue of the Virgin Mary with Jesus in her arms. Sometimes the candle will only burn out at one or two in the morning, long after she has started snoring.

Even if the Syrian were to come for me, how would he get past her door? She is like Cerberus, she sees everything, she hears everything, too, even when she's snoring. Once, when I was home for the holidays and my mother was inland, my father came to the gate and made a fuss. He threatened Maude, and shouted, and said that he would bring the police. But she only shouted back. She picked up a stick and threatened to hit him with it. After that, my mother bought a thicker padlock, and had a new wrought-iron fence put in, with sharp, curved spikes along the top.

I take off my pyjamas, and open the curtains. The moon is

shining through the mango tree, dappling the whole room. Even though it is the hot season, I am shivering under the sheet. I have forgotten about common rubbish, forgotten entirely. It is the Syrian now who slides along the passage, past Maude's door, whether or not the candle is burning. It is he who comes into my room without making a sound, and stands like a god at my bedside. Little by little, he folds back the sheet as I sleep. And then he just stands there in the moonlight, gazing. Long before he puts out a hand to touch my skin, he stands there looking at me. I want him never to grow tired of looking.

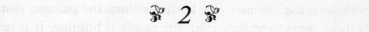

🌸 2 🌸

When the Syrian comes for me, it is not at all as I have dreamed it. He arrives at the gate, and rings the bell, tries to explain to the gardenboy that he has left his valise, which is true. I noticed it on one of the verandah chairs after breakfast, and carried it down to the summerhouse to examine its contents. The valise itself is a beautiful brown leather, with leather lining and black leather piping. Inside are shipping papers, and a fountain pen that I tried out on a leaf.

I watch him from behind the voiles of the study window, holding the valise to my chest. He is nothing like the man on the verandah. He is wearing a suit and a hat, and he is shouting above the racket of the dogs. I could easily go out to the gate, climb up onto the fence and pass the valise over to him. Maude has gone off to the supply store for coconut. Before my mother left, she told Maude to make jam tarts for my tea. She also promised to take me to the early show tonight, if she returned home in time, and to dinner afterwards at the Tudor Room.

The Syrian is waving his arms, pointing and shouting. But

the gardenboy shakes his head. He does not understand, and anyway, they are all frightened of strange men when my mother and Maude are away. He holds up a hand to tell the Syrian to wait, and runs around to the kitchen to find the housegirl. She will not come to find me. She will go straight to the gate, and tell the Syrian that he must wait for Maude to come back, that no one but Maude has the key to the padlock. My mother keeps every key to the house on a ring attached to her bag. When she goes inland, she hands the ring over to Maude.

I slip off the windowsill. In ten minutes, Maude will come singing around the corner of Princess Alice Road. She always sings when my mother is out of earshot. My mother says her high-pitched warbling hits her in the bone. But Maude sings anyway. When my mother is home, Maude can only warble softly as she cooks and as she moves along the passages.

I race to the hall window. When Maude turns the corner and sees my father's car, her warbling will turn into a scream. She will run down the hill like a wild woman. And when my mother hears the story, there will be no more talk of my going to university. "I can teach you everything you need to know in life," she will say. And when my father tells her that she is mad, that he will have the authorities after her, she will just laugh. "Go ahead!" she will say. "Why not?" And I will stay locked up here until I am too old and too ugly to matter anymore.

I take the valise and run through the lounge, out to the verandah and down the steps. As I come around to the front of the house, the housegirl is lumbering along the path from the kitchen. When she sees the valise in my hand, she begins to scream. She calls for the gardenboy to help, but he has gone to have his lunch. She calls for Maude, for Mrs. Holmes. "Aiiii!" she screams. "Aiiii!"

I reach the gate before her. It is already open, the chain has been cut and is hanging loose, with the padlock still on it. The dogs are out and barking at the driver.

"Ah, there you are," says the Syrian. "I was just coming for you." He takes the valise from me and throws it into the car, pushes me ahead of him. "Get in!" he says, climbing in behind me. "Go!" he says to the driver.

We roar down the hill and through the race course. The races are on, it is Wednesday, and the track has been laid over the road. But we are lucky. The booms are up and we can cross. Even the Umbilo lights are green, and there are no Indian buses double-parked outside the station. We speed over the railway tracks, down Commercial Road, right down to the docks. When we stop at the customs gate, the customs officer, crisp in his whites, looks into the car. He looks at me especially, and then at the Syrian. And then he checks something off and waves us through.

"Come," says the Syrian, getting out. "We don't have much time." We are right on the dock, right next to the gangway of a huge, grey ship.

It looms above us, dark and terrifying, with green slime on the sides and on the ropes that hold it in place. He leads me to the foot of the gangway. "Come on," he says.

But I stop. I refuse to go any farther. Once, my mother brought me to a ship to say goodbye to a friend she had known at the Conservatoire. We were to go on board and look around before it left, have tea up there, cakes, and ice cream. But the gangway terrified me, swaying high and loose over the water. The water itself was terrifying — dark and deep and oily. I stopped and would go no farther. They cajoled and they begged, they promised me a playroom with a rocking horse, a swimming pool, deck coits, everything wonderful. But when I looked down at that water, I could not consider stepping onto that gangway. And so my mother gave up and drove me home, very cross and threatening. I didn't care. We were together. We were safe.

The Syrian takes me by the elbow. "Come on," he says, pushing me ahead, moving me step by step. "One at a time." And so I climb, staring up at the dark opening ahead, at the shadowy creature who seems to be waiting for us up there. As we come closer, the shadow steps out into the light. It is my father. He reaches for me, pulls me to him, and kisses my forehead as he never has before. "There she is!" he exclaims. "There's my girl!" His eyes are glinting with delight. "Come along now, *tempus fugit*. I have the papers all ready."

"What papers?" I ask, stopping where I am. Suddenly, there is an ache across my heart for my mother. All the way in the car, even remembering that time when we were here before, I had forgotten her. But now I look out through the window at the far end of the foyer and I see the bay out there, silver in the midday sun, a few yachts sailing with the wind, free, and I think of her left behind.

"I can take you with me only if you are my wife," the Syrian explains.

I turn back to the entrance we have just come through. I could break loose and run down the gangway before they could even catch me. But what is out there except the years that lie ahead? Years of loving her, growing old by loving her? And her embroidering on as if my future were nothing but a lace-edged napkin to wave in the face of my father.

"Will you agree?" he asks.

"Of course she'll agree," my father says.

And I do. I nod.

"Good girl!" My father takes my arm and leads me through a door, into a small wood-panelled library. A man in a white uniform is waiting for us there.

"Ah, Captain," says my father, "here's the bride at last."

The Syrian puts down his valise and folds me under his arm. He smells like my father, wool and tobacco and Paco Rabane. And then suddenly the ache is gone and I am wishing that the girls at school could see me. We used to sit on our beds and guess who among us would be the first to marry. What would they say if they could see me now?

"All set?" My father has his pocket watch out. "Good! Sign here, and here. Exactly twelve miles out to sea, you'll be a married woman."

He hands the papers to the Captain, and then pulls a gold ring out of his pocket. "Here," he says, "you'll need this."

I try it on, but it is too small.

"Doesn't matter," the Captain says. "We can use mine. Any ring will do."

My father laughs. He is laughing as he kisses me goodbye, and when he walks down the gangway. "Ha! Ha!" he roars, and "Ha! Ha! Ha!"

3

And so it is done. I am to be married to a man whose name I do not know. My mother would laugh at this. Her laugh has attended every foolish thing in my life. But from now on and forever, I will remember her screams. I hear them just as the ship pulls away from the dock. They must have started when she drove into the garage and saw Maude standing there with the gate chain and padlock in her hand. She must have run past her, into the house and up the stairs, pulling herself by the banisters. When she saw I was not in my room, she would fly back out to the car, and then down to the docks, not stopping at the Umbilo light or at the customs gate either, but still arriving too late, too late. The gangway is up and the ship is pulling out. They have arranged everything perfectly between them, my father and his friend.

I sit on the bed with my hands over my ears, and he comes to sit next to me. He is saying things, but I can only hear her screams. The whole ship must be hearing them. They are horrible, horrible.

I jump up and run over to the porthole to look out. But we are on the wrong side of the ship, facing away from the dock. Still, I can see what I am leaving behind — a ship, another ship, and then the bluff, hazy in the heat. Her screams are blending now into a wail with the cries of the gulls. And then, when the engines roar into life, I lose her altogether.

He is calling me over, calling me back, but I am still deaf to him. I have deafened myself with crying. And I have completely forgotten who he is and why I came here with him. I have forgotten everything but what I have left behind.

"Would you like a piece of fruit?" he shouts.

We have three cabins to ourselves in a suite. There are bowls of flowers everywhere, a large basket of fruit and nuts.

I shake my head, but he gets up anyway, selects two ladyfinger bananas, a bunch of litchis, some Brazil nuts, and a nutcracker, arranging them on a plate.

"Come now," he says, "sit here."

And I do. I sit on the bed while he peels a litchi and holds it to my mouth. Litchis are my favourite, how does he know that? When they come into season, my mother goes down to the Indian market to buy them pink and fresh. She tells the servants to take the old brown ones for themselves.

But now all that is over. And even though the flesh is as fragrant as flowers under my nose, I shake my head.

"Come on," he says, quite sternly.

But I will not, I cannot.

So he eats it himself, wipes his fingers carefully on the napkin. Then he reaches over to stroke my hair, lifts it, twists it up onto my head, and lets it fall. He runs the tips of his fingers lightly up my neck, around my ear. I am half dizzy with his touch now, with the idea of his touch, too. He could be anyone, any stupid man with his fingers on my neck, and I would be dizzy like this, drunk like this. I would even urge him further, pull him down to me, dig my fingernails into his flesh as if I wanted to kill him. I *would* kill him if I had to. I would bite him, I would scream out.

He lays me back against the arm of the couch and takes off my sandals, caresses my feet. But when he slides his hands up my legs, I remember my mother in her blue silk, and I force my knees away from him. "No!" I say, sitting up. "Stop it!"

That is all I need to do. He drops his eyes for a minute and breathes deeply. Then he smiles and says, "We have half an hour till the wedding, and then the whole long journey of our lives."

But, hours or years, I know I must always be wary, or I will be his forever. I must lock the door between the cabins and sleep in here. If he finds ways to come to me in the night, if he tries to trick me with wine and presents, I must always be waiting for him, I must never give in.

After two nights at sea, the ship stops. In the distance is a bay, blue in the morning mist, with mountains behind it and a city spread out along their base.

"Come," my husband says, "we are going ashore." He is wearing a linen suit and a Panama hat, and he is in a hurry.

I follow him to the side of the ship. The Captain is waiting there for us. Far below, a motor launch bobs in the water. But the sea is rough and the wind is blowing, and we have to climb down a steep laddered stairway to reach it. I hold tight on to the railing and shiver. "No," I say, "I can't do it."

The Captain steps up. "You will have to carry her," he says to my husband. "Or would you prefer me to?"

My husband comes over to me then. "I won't let you fall," he says. "You have to trust me."

But still I shake my head. And so he wraps himself around me, uncurling my fingers from the railing one by one. He holds my hands inside his own and says, "I'm taking you down." And then he lifts me over his shoulder like a sack and carries me over to the steps.

I do not struggle. As he begins to climb down, I close my eyes, almost asleep with the thought of death, and with his warmth around me. He is saying things to comfort me as we descend, but he has the brim of his hat gripped between his teeth and I can only hear him as a murmur under the roar of the wind and the cries of the gulls, the slapping of the water against the ship. When we are at the bottom, he hands me to the man in the boat. And then he sits down next to me on the bench, saying nothing.

I should be glad, I know I should be glad that I am to be sent home so soon. But, now that it is happening, I only want to beg him to reconsider. I want to tell him that I need time, that I could try to be a wife, or I could decide to go home, I just need time to consider. I look over at him, searching for the words to say this, but he is staring grimly into the wind, his hat on his lap and his black hair whipped around his face. When he sees that I am shivering, he takes off his jacket and wraps it around me. But he doesn't pull me to him, he only asks, when we reach the dock, whether I am good at making up my mind quickly.

I shake my head. I am not good at it, I have never been good at it.

"Then I shall have to make it up for you," he says. He waves to a driver who is waiting next to a car on the dock. He takes my hand, leads me up the steps. "Littlefields," he says to the driver, "and get a move on, will you?"

I sit as far as I can from him in the car, staring out of the window, sullen and slumped. I don't ask him what Littlefields is, I don't even notice what we are passing. I only want to go back to the ship, and I don't know how to tell him this.

"Where are we going?" I say at last. The car has slowed down in the traffic now. Throngs of shoppers, and delivery boys, and men in suits and hats move along the pavements.

"Stop here!" he says to the driver. "Come on," he says to me, climbing out. He takes my hand and leads me through the crowd, into a dark, grand entrance, with "Littlefields" over the door.

"We need clothes for every occasion," he says to the saleslady in Better Dresses. "All seasons, all purposes. And we don't have much time." He sees that I have stopped sulking, and smiles, and pats me on the shoulder, just as my father does. "There's my girl," he says.

I shrug. I cannot bear him to think that I am pleased. And so, as the saleslady brings out the clothes one after another, I begin to be less pleased. It is my mother who should be sitting here next to me. She would know just what to wave off because it was too old for me, or too loud, or too anything. She would silence the saleslady's prattle by simply turning a skirt inside out to show her how shoddily the seams have been sewn.

But she is not here, and they are both looking at me, waiting for me to choose what to try on. There are pleated skirts and long skirts, blouses with gold buttons, blouses with tiny tucks, jerseys and tweed suits, dresses and slacks and twinsets. The saleslady has hung them all on a special rack and wheeled it in front of me. I stare at the clothes, trying to think, trying to remember.

"Will you choose now?" my husband says. "Or perhaps you will allow the saleslady to help you? We need to hurry."

I shrug again. What does the saleslady know about the way gold buttons can cheapen a blouse? Or what colours don't go with my skin? I don't even know myself. "I'll try them all on," I say.

And then, following her to the dressing room, I decide that I will simply keep them all anyway, even the ones I don't like, even cheap shorts that show off too much bottom. Who is to stop me now? Who is to care?

"Just ring the bell if you need me," she says. She has hung the clothes on two racks, placed the jerseys neatly on the chair.

As soon as the door shuts, I reach for the black chiffon evening dress with ostrich feathers around the hem. I have never been allowed to wear black before, I have never even had a proper evening dress. I slip my feet into the pair of high-heeled mules, there for trying on. And then I stand in front of the mirror staring at myself. I twist around and look over my shoulder.

"Knock-knock!" the saleslady says, "here come the coats. The gentleman says he's in a hurry. Oh my!" she cries, stopping in the doorway to look at me.

I turn to her and lift my chin. I have taken my ponytail down. My hair sweeps down over one cheek, black and sleek.

"I have the alteration hand waiting," she says. The simper is gone. She is looking at me properly now. "Will you need the waist taken in an inch or two?"

I reach for a camel's hair coat and put it on, stroking the fur at the collar and cuffs.

"Those can be taken off for cleaning," she says. "And you can button it to the neck, see? And turn up the collar like this."

The coat is beautiful, even my mother would have to say so. I turn to see the back of me, and then the front again.

"Come out so that the gentleman can see," she says.

But I slip my hands into the pockets of the coat and look at her in the mirror. "I'll keep it," I say. "I'll keep everything. Go and tell the gentleman that."

After he has taken me shopping, my husband seems to feel more like a husband. Every day, he comes into my cabin, every day he fondles my neck, my ears, my feet. But when he moves his hands to my knees, I sit up, and he bows his head. And even so, I can hear my mother laugh. "What sort of a man would bow his head to a girl?" she would cry. "A nonentity! A fool!"

But I would tell her that everyone here, even the Captain, bows to my husband. They stop him in the passage and ask if everything is to his liking. There are only nine passengers — a family of Brazilians and us — and even they bow to him. My husband has suggested that I join the Brazilians at the pool in the mornings because they have a daughter about my age and soon it will be too cold to swim. But they are oiled and noisy, and I prefer to look down on them from the deck above. Or to explore the ship barefoot, like a boy.

Except for the living areas and the pool, the ship is ugly, and the decks are narrow. On the lower decks, there is only a chain to keep you from falling over the side. Every now and then, passing from one end of the ship to the other, I swing out on the chain and look down at the sea boiling below. Ever since the climb down the ladder to the launch, I have come to love this sort of danger, I have even sought it out.

One morning, when I am up there, the Brazilian girl climbs up to sit next to me. She points down at the sailors, and says which one she would choose if she could. She would take the short one with blond hair and very bad teeth. I point to the tall waiter with a slight harelip, black eyes, black hair. When he comes out to the pool with his tray, he cannot help looking up at me. He watches me in the dining room, too, and sometimes I even look back. It is he I think of now when I dress in the morning, and when I put on lipstick. Sometimes, I lie naked in bed at night, thinking of him coming to see me lying there. It is nothing like the dreams of common rubbish that I used to have. He is real, and I am married.

After lunch, when the wind is up and the Brazilians stay indoors, I go out to the pool. I stand at the railing, looking down into the dark, deep furrow of water that is following us north. How could we have gone on the way we were, my mother and I, like a pair of lovers? Surely, surely I would have had to find a way to be taken from her sooner or later? Or even ripped from her as I have been, like a baboon — one minute a young female picking grubs out of her mother's fur, and, the next, snatched off into a future, screeching.

At the convent, I kept a photograph of her on my bedside table. It was as if I had two mothers — the one in that photograph, smiling down at me like a normal mother, holding my hand as we walked through town on a Saturday morning, and the other with her ring of keys and her furious shouting. When I came home for the weekend, I brought the photograph with me, and kept it on my bedside table, and kissed it every night. "She's here now," Maude would say, "so why you have to go and smudge the glass?"

I wish now that I had the photograph with me here. Staring down into the deep furrow of water, I cannot remember her smile anymore. All that I can think of is the slam of the front door when she comes home from rehearsal, the shout of my name, and then louder if I do not answer quickly enough.

I turn back to the pool, to the ship, silver in the afternoon light. If my mother would only listen, I would tell her that even if I have a husband who bows to me and buys me whatever I want, she is always with me. When I look in the mirror, it is she who is behind me, looking too. She is the one who decides which dress I wear to lunch, and which to dinner, she who tells me when I look cheap, and to stop showing off with the coat, it is still too hot to wear it. And even then, I lift my chin to her and smile. I want her to know that when I come home again, everything will be different. I will keep my own keys, and I will let myself in and out whenever I want to. If my father is coming to dinner, I will say, I'm going to be out tonight. Where? Just out.

I go back to the cabin, happy for a minute. There are my dresses hanging in the wardrobe just like her dresses. The jerseys are folded like hers, too, and the shoes tipped forward in a row. But her dresses were made specially for her, one by one, by the best dressmaker in the country. She ordered the material from England, and she took it inland to the dressmaker when she went to Katzenbogen. Every week, she had fittings there, until the dress was perfect. And when she brought it home, all wrapped in tissue paper, she hung it in her dressing room and we had to wait until after dinner to take out the pins and fold back the paper and gasp.

What could my clothes be, compared to this? Even my black chiffon. Even my coat. They could have been bought for anyone, any cheap bit of rubbish in a size 34 who would run off with a man because he told her she was beautiful.

When my husband comes to fetch me for tea, I shout all this at him. I pull the clothes from their hangers and throw them onto the floor, the coat too. Everything he has bought for me is hateful, I shout, even the coat. When I begin to throw the shoes, he comes over and holds my arms still. "You were promised to me, almost from the start," he says. "You have been mine for many, many years."

But the thought of the theft is unbearable now. So is the slimming salon, and the fruit bowl, and the Indian market, and the stupid way I sat up on the verandah wall, thinking he looked like a god.

"Who is my father to promise me to anyone?" I shout. "He is a nonentity! He is the *King* of Nonentities!"

I break away from him and slam into the bathroom, bolt the door. Then I sit on the stool, wondering what to do next. Locking myself away from him is not enough. He will just wait for me to come out again. I look around. His paisley dressing gown hangs from the hook on the door as usual. I take it down and throw it on the floor, stamp on it, jump on it.

But then I see his razor and I unscrew the blade. I pick up the gown and cut the tassels off the cord. I cut the cord itself in half, cut a big slash down the front. The cabin door opens and shuts, and I slide the bolt and look out. He has gone. I go to my wardrobe and pull out my coat, hang it on the door. Then I slice off the buttons, beautiful bone buttons, and I take them through to his cabin, and lay them on his pillow. I leave the blade there as well.

Then I throw the coat over my shoulder, I grab an armful of clothes, anything that I can carry, and I take them up the back stairs and onto the deck, to the railing behind the pool. A sailor is standing on my high perch, smoking, but I don't care. I pitch everything over the railing, and watch them flutter down, float for a while before they disappear into the wake. And then I close my eyes into the sea spray. I lift my face to the sun. "See?" I say to her. "See?"

When my husband comes back from tea, I am lying on my bed, naked. When I demanded separate cabins that first night on the ship, he immediately ordered the steward to arrange things that way. He does not care what the steward thinks, he does not care what anyone thinks about him. Before I go to bed, I bolt the door between our cabins. But I do not really need to. He never comes in without knocking. And he has never seen me without my clothes on.

He stares down at me now in silence. If I were at my desk, writing my letters as usual, he would kiss the top of my head and go through to his cabin to sleep. I would hear the buttons clink into his hand, into the wastepaper basket. And I would understand that he has expected worse from me. He has expected me to beg the Captain to stop the ship, to call the police, to annul this marriage and restore me to my mother.

"I knew you could not fail to be beautiful," he says. "I knew your father, and I had seen your mother, too."

I look up at him. I cannot say, "My mother is not beautiful," because I cannot say her name to him. And I know that it is my father who is to blame for everything. My mother was right, she has always been right. "Except for death," she said, "there are no mistakes in life. There are those who are to blame, and those who are not. But there are no mistakes in life."

"You are a beautiful woman," he says.

But the words are nothing to me now. I turn my head away, hopelessly naked under his gaze. "Go away!" I say. But I don't really want him to go, I want a fight. I roll onto my side to face the wall, and he comes to sit on the edge of the bed. He lays his hand on my hip, begins stroking my side, down into my waist and up again, higher and lower, until he has touched my breast with his fingers, he has his hand around it, and the other around my bottom, around my thigh. He is stroking me so lightly that I have to force my eyes open, force myself up from the deepest mud at the bottom of the sea and draw in my legs away from him.

"Let me keep my hand there," he says.

I shake my head.

"Why?" he says. "Is it because you are frightened?"

I shake my head again. I will not tell him why. Even if I could find the words, I cannot utter them to him. At dinner, I can talk to the Captain, or to the Chief Engineer. And sometimes I talk to the Brazilian girl. When she asked me where my father and I were going, I did not correct her. I told her we were going to a big villa that we have, with a garden, and two dogs. But her mother always calls her away when she talks to me. As my own mother would, too.

At Rio, the Brazilians leave the ship, and my husband has to go on shore for a meeting. He will return for lunch, he says, and then we will go into the city together, all around the sights. He has asked me to stay in the cabin while he is gone, and to lock the doors. He has said this respectfully, and told me that the cabin steward will be in the passage outside, in case I need anything. I know that the cabin steward has been placed there to stop me running away. But what would be the point of running away? All my papers are locked in the safe. And anyway, where would I go? And why?

As soon as he is gone, I open the door to ask the cabin steward to bring my breakfast. But it is not the cabin steward at all, it is my waiter standing there. We look at each other for a moment. And then I find a way to say that I want brown toast, and a glass of guava juice, and tea.

Waiting for him to return, I stand in the middle of the room, staring into the mirror. I am in my dressing gown, pink and cream and tied at the waist. I still have most of the things my husband bought me, but they are just clothes again, even this gown that I chose because it was silk, like my mother's, and expensive. I turn, and lift my chin, and toss my hair back like her. I open the sash and shrug off the gown. I am brown from the sun, beautifully curved.

When the waiter knocks, I call him in. He stops when he sees me naked, closes the door behind him.

"Put the tray in there," I say.

"Here?" He is staring boldly at me now, my breasts, my hips. He smiles, but I see that his lip is quivering.

People are walking down the passage, talking, shouting. He glances at the door, but I beckon him to me. I don't care who could walk in, I don't care about anything. I reach up to undo the top button of his jacket. He smells of sweat and hair oil, and fried food, and I laugh because I cannot undo the button, it is too tight. He doesn't laugh with me. He pushes me away, running his fingers down the buttons like a spider. He throws the jacket off, and then his shirt, unbuckles his belt, kicks off his shoes, his trousers, everything flung away.

And then he stares down at himself so that I have to stare down, too. He looks strange and ridiculous, and I want to laugh. I do laugh. I reach over to touch him, but he grasps me by the arms and pushes me down to the floor, right there among his clothes. He holds me down there while he kneels over me, opening my thighs with one knee.

"Wait," I say, but he doesn't wait. He begins to jab at me, jabs and jabs so that I cry out. "Stop it!" I say.

He stops for a moment, panting like a dog. But then he starts again, pushing himself at me, pushing and pushing until he is burning into me like fire, grunting and lunging and thrusting like one of our dogs. I have my fingers in his flesh to hold on to the pain, to hold it away from me for a moment, but I can't, and I ask him, I beg him to stop. And then, at last, he cries out himself, and sinks his head onto my shoulder, and it stops.

Outside, someone is playing a concertina. Women are laughing, and there is the smell of rotting fruit, rotting fish. I am ashamed now of screaming, I want to tell him so. But he won't even look at me. I want to ask him to forgive me, I don't know for what. I want to ask my mother to forgive me too. When I think of her, I begin to cry again. I want to tell her that I am still hers, not his. Just look at him lying there, sneering up at the ceiling with his harelip and his flash of teeth. How could I be his forever? I am married. I have a husband.

And then remembering this, remembering everything at once, I know, in this moment, that my husband has wanted this to happen. That he has made it happen.

❧ 4 ❧

After Rio, the waiter disappears. No one says anything to me about this, and there is no one to ask. Everything goes back to the way it was before, except that my husband does not try to stroke me anymore. He does not come into my cabin at all. And the cold weather has come.

Every day, I write to my mother. I tell her we have separate bedrooms, and that I bolt my door at night. I tell her about the coat, too, and the clothes and shoes I threw into the water. I want to make her laugh. I want us to laugh at him together.

Every morning, I fetch an envelope and some paper from the library, a few sheets at a time. When I have finished a letter, I seal it and zip it into the pocket of my handbag. He must know that I write the letters. Since the waiter came to my room, I have caught him watching me in a different way, the way you watch an ant make its way up and down a stalk of grass. Perhaps he is waiting for me to look at him the way I looked at the waiter. But every time I think of the waiter now,

I am ashamed. And I am glad that he is gone. He was rude and rough and he is nothing to me.

As we move farther north, I begin to wonder what my husband's villa is like. My mother grew up in a house with a tennis court and a glassed-in conservatory, glass-fronted bookcases, lilacs in the garden, and a ball every New Year's Eve. During the War, their money was hidden away, like her. The Nazis turned everything upside down, looking for it, but they never found it. She found it herself, just where her father had told them all to look. Blood money, she says, it will never be enough for what has been taken away. Never.

And now I have been taken from her too, and how will she forgive me? I cry as I write this to her. When I come to lunch, my eyes are red.

"Dearest child," says my husband, "how can I help you?"

I look away. His voice is soft, and the words make me want to give up. I want to let him put his arms around me, to fall asleep in his arms. Since the waiter came to my cabin, I have lost the gift of sleep. Every night I wake in the dark with my heart beating wildly. I listen to the engine of the ship grinding us north, and I think of my mother in her satin bed jacket, having breakfast on a tray. Or putting on her makeup at her dressing table. Or in her dressing room, always brilliant in the morning sunlight.

Her clothes hang there in perfect order — highest to lowest — and the shoes are all tipped forward in rows. The dresses for her performances hang in a separate wardrobe — the magenta silk with the long train, and the black taffeta, and the cream that is really a pale, pale pink, the same colour as my dressing gown. Her clothes look alive hanging there, with the sleeves and the bodices stuffed with tissue paper, and the skirts laid out along a white sheet. Every week, I hear Maude singing as she hangs them out to air on the sleeping porch, and sometimes I go out too, just to look at them there, just to think about my mother in them.

Sometimes she gives me the key to her jewelry drawer and lets me take out all the boxes, and open them, and choose what to try on. Once she left her drawer open by mistake, and I took them all out and put them on as usual. And then I thought of trying on her strapless taffeta and her high-heeled diamanté sling-backs, just to see how they would look. I put on her ostrich feather cape, too, and her long kid gloves, and I dabbed Madame Rochas behind my ears. I went through to her bathroom and put on some rouge and lipstick and mascara and even a beauty spot high on my right cheek. When she came home and called for me, I went to the top of the stairs and waited.

Then I lifted the skirt and started to go down. But when she saw me, she screamed, and Maude came running. So I started screaming, too, we were all screaming. "Sorry!" I shouted, "Sorry, Ma!" But she had grabbed my arms and wouldn't let go, spitting her words at me, spitting them into my face. "Thief! Tart! Trollop!"

The night before we arrive in America my husband gives me a leather box. It is my eighteenth birthday. "Open it," he says, "I bought it for you in Rio."

Inside is a double string of pearls with an emerald-and-diamond clasp, and pearl drop earrings to match. The pearls are bigger than my mother's black evening pearls. They are beautiful and gleaming and I long to put them on. But I hand the box back. "I don't have pierced ears," I say. "My mother says only cheap girls pierce their ears."

Ah, he says, in some countries all women pierce their ears, even young girls, even babies. But if I like, he will have the earrings changed, or I can have my ears pierced, whichever I wish. He hands the box back to me. "Please keep it," he says. "You don't have to wear them if you don't want to."

That night, I wear the pearl necklace to dinner. I know that he will not make a point of noticing it. He will only ask me, as usual, to join him and the Captain in the lounge after dinner. Usually, I go back to the cabin to write my letters, but now I agree to stay, and I agree to a cognac too. The pearls are warm, and heavy as stones around my neck, and I want to cradle the snifter in my hand.

The Captain is talking about the weather. It is raw, he says, the airports are closed. And the wind only makes things worse. The end of the world will come with wind, he says.

My husband has never mentioned the coat since the day I cut off the buttons and threw it into the sea. But now I wonder how I will manage without it. Outside, the wind blows snow all around the ship, up against the windows. It is dark and grey and horrible.

I take a sip of cognac. The liquid burns down my throat, into my thighs, right down to my ankles. My cheeks are burning, too, and when my husband reaches for my hand, I let him take it.

The Captain is saying that he lives on an island in the English Channel, where the weather is milder. His wife is a weaver, he says, although she is no Penelope, he can assure us of that, ha!

I say that I detest winter and winter clothing. It is hard to breathe in it, I feel like an Eskimo.

"Winter has unleashed her tongue," says my husband, squeezing my hand.

He is right. The cognac has let me forget how to be silent with him. It has let me forget everything but the two men sitting forward to listen to me. And so I tell them the story of the coat and the buttons — every detail of the destruction except the reason why.

The Captain smiles, but he is watching my husband. Perhaps he thinks that I should be punished, that my husband is a fool not to punish me.

"Penelope is a drip," I say, "with all that weaving and unweaving. Why didn't she just accept one of those lovers? Or send them all away? It makes no sense at all to me."

"'It little profits that an idle king —'" says my husband.

"'By this still hearth —'" I add.

"Go on!" he cries. "Go on!"

And so I do. I lift my chin and deliver the whole poem to them as if I were on the stage at school. When it is over, my husband calls the steward over for more cognac. "Three," he says, without even asking.

I take a gulp of the second glass. My head is spinning now, and my stomach has turned sour with the fright of the performance. I try to stand, to say good night, but I fall back into the chair with a laugh. My husband offers me his arm. I need it to steady myself, to lead me between the tables, out of the lounge, and down the stairs, along the passage to our cabin.

"I should not have given you so much cognac," he says, bolting the outside door. "But I'm glad I did."

I flop onto the bed and look up at him and smile, "The As-syrian came down like a wolf on the fold." I have been wanting to say this ever since the day he first came to our house. But it was impossible then, and it has been impossible since.

He sits down next to me and wraps me in his arms. "You are mine," he says. "Do you understand that?"

I nod. But I do not understand. I lean against him, and close my eyes, and let him lift my chin and kiss me on the mouth. He lays me back on the bed, and takes off my shoes, my skirt, my stockings, as if I were a baby.

I watch him take off his own clothes, and I stare at the black hair curling over his chest, down his legs. He is brown all over, massive and wonderful. When he comes to lie with me, he is soft as a bear, and warm. I run my fingers through his hair and laugh.

He seems to be laughing, too. But then he wipes an arm across his eyes and I see that he is crying. He does not even mind that I see this. He just looks over at me as if he has asked me a question.

"Close your eyes," I say to him. And even though I am still burning, I lift myself over him, onto him. I laugh as he throws back his head and clenches his teeth, and soon my pain becomes a sort of pleasure, a sort of urgency that will not stop, that I never want to stop. And then, suddenly, he reaches for me and pulls me down with a wild force, stopping me completely, shouting, "Forgive me! Oh, forgive me, darling!"

And only then do I remember my mother, and I know that it is too late, I have let it happen. I pull myself away from him and begin to cry, terrible gasping sobs.

"Darling," he says. "Come here. *Please!*"

I try to push him away, but he is strong. He folds himself

around me, pulls me down to him, strokes me and kisses me. "It takes time," he says. "I promise you, darling, I promise that it will be wonderful."

But all the time in the world will not undo what I have done now. I might as well be a murderess. I might as well go to jail and never see her again. She was right, she is always right. He has finished what the waiter began. And now I will be his forever.

✤ 5 ✤

It is said that the dying are jealous of life. But Nalia is jealous only of the dead. Her dead. She is furious with their silence, furious with herself for being coughed back out of that stinking pit and into a life sentence.

And yet she had struggled to be coughed out. She had chewed on a piece of leather strap, swallowed it, chewed and swallowed. On the day of liberation, she had listened when Katzenbogen said, Eat very slowly, little by little. With her insides torn to nothing by the dog of hunger, she had taken one small bite, and then waited.

But now she will eat nothing. Nor will she drink. Maude sits on a straight-backed chair next to the bed, watching. If Nalia dies, what will become of her own life? Who will consider a housekeeper after eighteen years in the employ of a mad-woman?

"What if she comes back?" Maude says. "She won't have a mother." She has said this several times.

"Stupid cow!" Nalia whispers. "Why don't you shut up?"

"But you're punishing your own child."

"Shut up."

Maude has already been down to the docks twice, two buses and a long walk to the father's office there. But both times she was turned away by the scarecrow behind the desk. She even phoned Dr. Slatkin. He just said, "Try Coca-Cola." And then, the next time she phoned, he said, "If this is what she wants, there is nothing anyone can do, Maude."

"Sack the staff," Nalia says. "Take the money out of my locked drawer and pay them for three months. I want them gone by tomorrow."

"And me?"

"You will sit here and watch me die."

"Don't be silly now. Have a sip of Coca-Cola."

That was last week. This week there is the sweet smell of death in the room. Nalia has begun to shiver. So Maude has closed the windows and the curtains to keep the Devil of death outside.

"Stop clacking those beads, for God's sake. They sound like false teeth."

Maude slips the rosary into her apron pocket and goes downstairs for her tea. No one has dusted the house, nothing is swept in the garden, the grass is unmowed. Yesterday, Mrs. Holmes phoned to find out if they were looking for a garden-boy, she could send hers over if they liked. Maude told her the madam was sick and couldn't bear the sound of a lawn mower. She would phone back when she got better.

As soon as Maude is out of the room, Nalia pushes herself up. She slips her legs over the side of the bed, holding on to the bedside table, trying to stand. But she sinks to the floor, she will have to crawl. She pulls her nightie over her head and throws it aside, and then drags herself along, hands and knees, her breasts swinging. When she reaches the bathroom, she stops for breath before she moves over the threshold, over the cold tiles, crawling to the toilet, panting like a dog.

She grasps the seat with both hands, trying to push it up, pushes and pushes until it stays there. Then she hangs her chin and her arms over the porcelain edge. She is shivering violently now, but she lifts herself into the bowl, tips herself over the edge and down, down towards the water. But she cannot go far enough, she cannot reach it. She rests her cheek against the porcelain and closes her eyes.

Perhaps, after all, it is easier to live than to die. She will just have to wait, like everyone else. She will have to lie here and wait for it to come to her. And even so, that coward, that murderer will know that this death is no mistake. He will know the reason why.

"Eeee! Ma'am! Aiiiii!" Maude has her like a vulture in her claws. So Maude is the one, then, who will finish her off, tear her apart, take what is left.

"Do it," Nalia says. "Do it now."

But Maude picks her up and carries her in her arms, like a child, back to bed. She wraps her in the mohair blanket and Nalia cannot help it — she cannot help the warmth around her body, the softness. She cannot help licking her lips when Maude wipes them with a wet cloth, licking and swallowing.

And then Maude is at the phone, dialling. "Mr. Braughton, it is Maude speaking, Mrs. Nalia's housekeeper. Please, Master, madam is very, very sick, please call the father of the child. Yes, we got a doctor, but he won't come. Please?"

Braughton? Why Braughton? Braughton was the one who gave her top billing, even when she was an unknown, a nothing herself.

"Braughton doesn't deserve this," she whispers.

"No one deserves this," says Maude. "Not even you."

When the girl's father arrives, the dogs don't bark. They follow him upstairs in a rush, right into the bedroom and up to the bed. He picks up her wrist and takes her pulse, puts it gently back.

"For God's sake, Maude," he says, "open the curtains and the windows." He sits on the edge of the bed and smooths Nalia's hair back from her forehead, like a lover. It is grey at the roots, something she never allows. "Don't you dare do this, Natalia," he says.

"Murderer!"

He stares at her, this furious woman, this thorn in his liver, and, for God's sake, he is close to tears. He had expected the fury and the screaming and the lawyers. He had even expected her to send Maude down to his office to beg. But this, but this — he lifts her hand again. It is light as a glove. The skin is loose, and the nail varnish chipped almost to nothing. "Natalia," he says, "I'll see what I can do to bring her back."

She tries to pull her hand away but he holds it firmly. So she turns her face from him, keeping her eyes shut. It is no wonder to him that this woman survived as she did, never has been. He has used her story mercilessly on his other women, as if he had written it himself.

He glances around the room. He hasn't been up here since the child was born. It needs paint. So does the house. She should have the ivy pulled off, the whole thing plastered and painted white. It should be a shining ship up here, with its pillared verandahs and green-striped awnings.

But he cannot tell her this. It is impossible to tell Nalia anything.

"If I can have it annulled, you can have her back," he says. He knows that the marriage is not yet a marriage. He has had a telephone call from the ship.

Nalia opens her eyes. "Murderer!" she whispers.

"Oh give it a rest, won't you?" After all, he can take no pleasure in any of this. "This performance of yours is vanity, Natalia," he says.

"Get out of my house!"

He stands up then, and so do the dogs.

"Follow him," she tells Maude.

But Maude stays in the green chair, watching him go. "The dogs will follow him," she says.

"Then you're sacked too."

"Too bad for that, hey?" Maude reaches for her knitting.

"You're getting cheeky," Nalia says. "And it's all because of him."

"Want some tea?"

"Yes. Lemon, not milk."

And so it is over. At first, the trays come up every hour or so, tea and Coca-Cola and broth. Then there are rusks, then stewed apple, then giblet soup. Nalia asks for her bedjacket, and extra pillows so that she can sit up and read the paper. She has the hairdresser come to the house, and she agrees that Mrs. Holmes may send her gardenboy over, although she is not to come herself, no one is to come to the house.

Every evening the phone tings next to her bed, and Nalia knows that it is Maude in the breakfast room, dialling the murderer's number. She picks it up and hears her tell him what has been eaten that day, what ordered for tomorrow, and that they have the housegirl back now, but not the gardenboy.

Nothing, nothing will ever be right again. Even Maude has gone over to the enemy. And yet all Nalia can think of are his words. *If I can have it annulled, you can have her back.* He is worse than a dog — he is a murderer and a thief — but she must take her hope now from a dog. This is what happens in life. It will happen to the girl, too, and there is nothing she can do about it, nothing. But, oh — oh, she wants her back. Wanting life is nothing to this, nothing at all. What is life? A burden, a trial. If he is right, if it is vanity to want to die, then surely this is lust, wanting to live only for her daughter's return? Let him throw any words he likes at her. Let him speak for hours on the phone to Maude. What is he more than a thief and a dog himself? He is nothing. He is the King of Nothing. But he is the only one who can bring the girl back.

Once she is up and dressed and coming downstairs, it is as if she has been on a long journey. She sees that everything is shabby and dull and she has the servants take the carpets out and beat them. She gives Maude a list of things to do. The floors are to be washed and waxed properly, for once. The brasses on the stairs are to be polished again, no traces left of Brasso. The curtains are to be taken down and washed. Lampshades and slipcovers and the cushions on the dining room chairs — everything is to be brushed or washed or measured for replacement.

Now that Nalia is out of bed, Maude must go down to the phone box at the corner to deliver her reports to the father. One afternoon, Nalia drives down there herself. She stops the car and keeps her hand on the hooter so that people come out of their houses to see what the matter is, and Maude has to hang up. After that, Maude stays home. "You speak to him or you work for me," Nalia tells her. "Not both."

"He only wants what is best," says Maude, sulking.

"Don't be stupider than you look," Nalia says. Katzenbogen was right after all, she thinks. Who *is* there to trust? Not Maude, not anyone.

"But he's trying to get her back for us."

"Idiot!" Nalia snaps. "Who do you think took her away in the first place?"

For the first time in eighteen years, Nalia does not go inland. Inland can wait, she says, and so can she. Since the end of the War, she has never lived one day in the future, hardly allowed herself a glimpse into that dim terrain. But now she is full of it, she is waiting for it every hour. She writes all this down in a notebook that she keeps in her bedside table. When she does go inland again, she will read it to Katzenbogen. She will have him know that she is now alive in the future. She is in love with it.

All those months after liberation, when they tramped from place to place, and he would argue a future for Mankind, on and on, she would stare at him — gaunt, ragged, hoarse — and she would laugh. "Just take a look at yourself," she would say. "Just take a look at me."

But now she goes down the passage to the girl's room full of hope. She turns the key and opens the door. Everything is the same in there, even the clothes left lying around on the spare bed, and those cheap cork wedges the girl had nagged for. She opens the wardrobe door wide. What was she wearing when she left? What dress? What shoes?

She sits down on the bed, losing a little hope, just a little. There is the hairbrush on the dressing table, and the bag of curlers, the diary, and, oh, that photograph in the filigree frame. She reaches over for it, sits with it on her lap. There is the ache across her heart again. A heart does ache, she thinks. Ache is the right word.

Why did the girl love this photograph so? What did she see in it? Saturday mornings, tea and a bun at the Bon Marché? And then a pair of shoes to find, a pencil box for school, a strapless bra? Was that all the girl's happiness? Was it nothing, nothing that she herself had kept her from the shoddy and the mediocre? That they had come this far together? This far?

She stares down at the picture. The photographer must have caught them hurrying home for lunch, the girl twisting back to look into Cottam's window, wanting something more, for a change. Had she wanted it so badly that she had to run away? Had Katzenbogen been right all along? Sooner or later, he had said, sooner or later.

She puts the photograph back on the bedside table. She will have Maude pack everything except the photograph into boxes, and mark them carefully, and put them under the house. When the girl comes back, she will want new clothes, grown-up things. Nalia will take her to town again, mother and daughter. Everyone will see them, Nalia will make sure of that. They will see the girl sitting in the front row of her mother's audience without Maude at her side, for once. And they will know she came back of her own free will, that she stays because she wants to. All of them will know who really won in the end.

Braughton has been over several times. From the start, it was Braughton who had warned her about the girl's father, but would she listen? Would she turn the man away when he came to her night after night? And when he started making excuses, when Braughton suggested that there might be another woman — other women all over the place — would she believe him then, either?

All along, Katzenbogen says, she understood about the girl's father and his women. She has spent her years since the War looking for punishment, he says, but what does he know? No doubt, he would say that she wanted that thief to come and take the girl away, too. Katzenbogen will say anything to blame her, anything at all. Except for death, he says, there are no mistakes in life. But what does he know? He was in the camp himself, and still what does he know?

❧ 6 ❧

He has brought me to an island, Ma. We came in a motor launch, straight from the ship. But there was trouble landing, everything covered in mist. And then, when the mist lifted, I forgot completely what I had imagined it would be like — villa and garden and dogs — because there was the island, steep and high, like a mountain rising out of the sea. The sea itself was calm all around, with bright sun, and boats in the distance. But even so the island was cold, bitterly cold and windy.

When you told me about winter, Ma, I thought only of the brightest whiteness, snow on everything, clean and lovely, and you sitting in the window seat with your grandmother, eating steamed puddings after supper. But it is nothing like that here. It is bare and stark, and also dark and damp, and yet it never snows, he says.

We took a funicular to the top of the mountain. It is his own funicular, his own island too. The funicular is furnished like an old-fashioned train compartment. The seats are covered in dark green velvet, with curtains and a Persian carpet. Looking down, you can see the houses built back from the water in a row — small whitewashed houses with corrugated iron roofs and walled gardens behind them. One, right on the waterfront, is taller than the rest, with a tiled roof and balconies. I asked him about it, but he pretended not to hear me. And then we lost sight of the town, we were moving up the mountain, which is quite bare except for scrub growing here and there, and a deep wooded chasm down the middle.

Once we reached the top, everything was different. It is flat up here, and green, and warmer. A shaded boulevard runs from the landing platform to the gates of the villa. A Land Rover was waiting for us when we arrived, but we could easily have walked. I wanted to walk, but he said no, there would be plenty of time for walking. And so we drove, the huge gates of his garden opening, and then closing behind us automatically.

His garden itself is as big as a park, Ma, with royal palms along the fence, and lawns, and a fountain too. On either side of the driveway is a grove of broad-leaved trees. They look like mangoes, but the leaves are rounder, and the fruit is small and orange, hanging in bunches like dates. As we drove in, I saw two white rabbits sitting in the fork of one of the trees. I did see them, but when I asked him, he just smiled. If he doesn't want to tell me something, it is as if I am speaking a language he does not understand.

All you can see of the villa from the garden is the massive front door under a stone archway, and shuttered windows on either side. When you go in, though, it is enormous, built down the cliff, with the bedrooms at the bottom and the mountain falling away under your feet. All of the rooms except the kitchen and his study look out over the sea on the other side of the mountain. When you look out there, it is as if the gardens in the front don't exist, because it is as bleak and bare as it was coming up. The villa is bleak, too, with its winding passages and stone stairways, and its large, gloomy rooms.

I have a whole suite to myself — bedroom, sitting room, dressing room. The bedroom is even bigger than yours. It is faded and frilly, and it smells stale, like an old woman. When I say this to him, he laughs. Perhaps he thinks I might be jealous, even of an old woman, but I am not. I am only jealous of the distance between you and me, which seems now to be bigger than the world.

As soon as we arrived, I asked him to show me a map so that I could know where I was. He brought one out and spread it across the table, but it showed only islands and depths and currents — any fool could see it was a shipping map. I shouted this at him. I tore it up and stamped on it and demanded a proper map. But he just shook his head. There are hundreds of islands like this, he said, it is impossible to tell one from another.

And so I don't know where I am at all. But, wherever it is, I have gone too far, Ma, you are never behind me anymore. At first I think you are silent because you are angry. And then I think, no, you are always angry; you must be dead. And so I cry bitterly. I lock the door of my room and will not come out when he knocks. I tell him that he has murdered you, he and my father, that he has turned me into a murderess too. He shouts through the door that he has had word from my father. You are fine, everyone at home is fine.

After this, it is only worse. I am jealous of your being fine, and angry too. I try to write all this to you, but I have to learn a new way to find the words. At home, when I wrote in my diary, it was as if you were reading as I wrote, laughing and scolding. But now you are silent. You are fine, and I am punished.

Sister Benedict was right. She always said I would be punished for my pride. When they would talk of the sufferings of Jesus, I'd lift my chin as if I knew all about it. Even now, I will not ask my husband for what I want. If it is a notebook to write in, I tell him that I had a diary at home, and a broad-nibbed fountain pen with special magenta ink that you brought me from inland. And then, the next time he comes back from the mainland, there they are on the hall table — notebook, pen, and ink. And even so, I am too proud to pick them up. So I leave them there for a day or a week, I don't even touch them. I wait until he isn't looking before I take them upstairs to my room. And only then do I open the notebook to smell the lovely fresh paper, to fill the pen with ink.

Everything here belongs to him, even the dogs. If I call them into my room and close the door, they sit with their noses to the threshold, sighing to be let out again. All they want is to lie at his feet and lick his shoes. He says that they will get used to me, and that there will be flowers in the spring, and birds, and the sun will be hotter than I could wish it. But still, there won't be hadedahs on the lawn, or spitting bugs singing in the jacarandas. We will not be able to sit on the verandah, you and I, watching the afternoon storm build up.

There are boats out on the sea, free and happy, and every few days there is a ship. I watch them from my terrace, I stare down at them as if they must see me here. But even if they could, what would they do? What do I want them to do?

Since that night on the ship, I have never let him back into my room, and he has never asked. I can see by the way he looks at me, though, that he is waiting. He watches everything I do. And so, I lift my hair onto my head and let it fall again. I push my chair back and stretch my legs out for him. I have learned how to turn up the heat so that I can walk around the villa in shorts and bare feet. The two sisters who work here make a show of fanning themselves and complaining, but I pay no attention, and he says nothing at all.

They arrive early every morning and leave again after supper. They are very ugly, with teeth missing and dyed black hair. I know that they laugh behind my back. When I tell him this, he says they are not laughing at me, they are laughing at him because he has a young and beautiful wife. But after that, the laughing stops and the villa is silent except for the sound of cleaning and the noises of the kitchen.

When he is away, the silence is terrible, Ma. At first, I slept night and day, and only woke up when one of the sisters knocked on the door because lunch was ready. And then, after lunch, I would sleep again until dinner. All that sleeping only left me more tired. I wandered along the corridors, staring into this room or that, but I didn't want to know anything about this place. I was only waiting for him to come back.

I can always tell from the dogs when he is returning. They go up to the front door and lie there, sometimes for hours, sometimes for days. And then, when I hear them bark, when I hear his car on the gravel of the driveway, I run to the hall window to watch him climb out. When I would watch for boys out of the car window, I would watch like this. But what was I looking for then, Ma? A boy? Or the idea of a boy? Seeing him there on the driveway in his hat and scarf, I don't know what I am looking for now, either. I only know that, even if he is nothing — even if he is the King of Nothing — I can't help it, Ma, I am glad to see him.

Today is Sunday and he has closed himself into his study. You and I would be going to hear the Africans singing at the river. And then up the coast for lunch. I would order a crayfish sandwich and you'd have the cheese and biscuit plate, with a pot of tea to follow. You'd put on a hairnet when the wind picked up, and come out onto the terrace to watch me swimming in the hotel pool.

He always listens to music on a Sunday. Usually it is Beethoven piano sonatas, but today it is Schubert lieder. I creep up there and fold myself silently onto the floor outside the door to listen. He must know I am there because the dogs always know. They sniff at me under the door. And yet, still, he doesn't come to find me. He wants me to do as I please, he says.

Listening now to the singer lifting and lifting through the song, I close my eyes and pretend that I am lying with our dogs under the piano at home, watching your foot poised over the pedal. What was so terrible about that, Ma? Every day I ask myself this question, but I only come back to these rooms, this strange winter place.

I am never hungry anymore, and my clothes are too big for me. I had to ask him for a safety pin to hold up my trousers. I have even forgotten how it felt to long for Maude's jam tarts or a second helping of lamb curry. When he asks me what sort of food I like, I cannot remember that either. "Curry," I tell him, "and jam tarts." And then, the next day or the next, there is curried chicken and some sort of berry tart for lunch. But they are nothing like ours, and as long as he is looking, I cannot eat anyway. Sometimes, at night, when the sisters are gone and he is away, I go down to the kitchen and find a tin of tomato juice there, or a jar of cashews. I carry them back to my room and eat them there. And then, the next day, there are bowls of cashews on the table, a jug of tomato juice.

The study door opens, and there he is, standing above me. "Won't you come in, Thea?" he says. He reaches down for my hand. "Come," he says, pulling me to my feet and into the room.

Oh Ma, how lovely it is in there! It smells of leather and cigars and dogs, and it is golden in the lamplight. There are prints on the walls, old prints of natives in tribal dress, and one of a lioness tearing into the carcass of a zebra. Even the curtains are like our curtains — floral linen, faded from the sun. There are Persian carpets, too, and a lovely leather divan.

"Shall I light a fire?" he says.

But it is warm in here already, soft in the lamplight. There is an ebony matchbox holder on the mantelpiece, inlaid with ivory, just like ours. Next to it is a photograph in a silver frame. I take it down and hold it to the light. It is of my father and him, both young, both dark as natives. And suddenly you are back, you are behind me saying, "Pinkerton and Sharpless! Ha!" I even turn to look for you. I even laugh.

"Tanganyika," he says, "when it was still Tanganyika."

And all of a sudden, that is where I want to be. Tanganyika. "Why can't we go there?" I say, trying not to cry. I can hear myself sounding like a child, wanting what I cannot have, and I turn to leave, although I don't ever want to leave this room. I want to ask him to put a bed in here for me. I want him to lock me in here when he goes away. I could wait in here all winter, Ma, and I could be happy.

He takes the photograph from me and puts it back on the mantelpiece. Then he offers me a bowl of cashews, he opens a liquor cabinet next to the fireplace, and I see rows of keys hanging there, sparkling and familiar.

"Would you like cognac?" he asks.

I shake my head, and he comes to take my face in his hands. He looks at me as he did at dinner that first night, and on the verandah before that. "All I want," he says, "is to make you happy."

I know you would laugh at this, but I believe him. I don't know who he is or why he wants to make me happy, but I let him lead me to the divan and lay me down there.

He kneels at my feet and begins to stroke them, and to kiss them. He kisses my calves, too, and my thighs, and I don't stop him at all. I let him lift my skirt. I let him kiss me and stroke me anywhere he likes, anywhere. I let him lift me to him, hold me there until I have to grab him, I have him by the hair. "Please!" I shout. "Please! Please! Please!"

After that, he stays home with me longer. And every day he is here, I go up to his study, sometimes twice, sometimes more. I cannot help it. I ask him not to bathe in the mornings because I like the smell of him without the strange island soap. I am drunk with the smell of him, and with his terrible need, and with my own. If I think of this in the night, I lie awake, waiting for the morning. But I will not go to him in his bedroom, nor will I have him in mine. Even though I am his wife, it is not as his wife that I go up to his study. It is as someone I have never been before, Ma, not even in my dreams. When I am with him in there, I am furious and grasping. I am helpless and abject and shameless. And my father is wrong. The stinking swamp is not marriage at all. It is up there, in that study. What is marriage anyway, but a form of theft? Someone taken, someone left behind. But with this, I am his, I will always be his. And I know there is no way back.

7

Nalia drives fast through the racecourse and up the hill, up and up, trying, as usual, to surprise herself with the sight of the house as the girl will see it. The painters are gone now, and the new awnings are up, the palms have been trimmed, and the cannas are blooming along the fence. It is perfect. That is what the girl will write in her diary. She will write, "The house is perfect, a gleaming white castle." She will write, "I am home and it is perfect."

Nalia hoots for Maude to open the garage. Perhaps they should go to the mountains over Christmas and New Year, get away from the throngs who come down to the coast for their holidays. She knows that the girl might choose to be there, among the throngs, that she will grow up and want a life of her own perhaps. Nalia has even written these words in her notebook so that she can try to believe them. She has written them and she has read them, but still they are nothing. They are only words.

Maude stretches the phone cord to the window. "Master," she says, "Madam is hooting."

"Well, let her hoot."

"But, master, how am I going to say it?"

"Oh come now, Maude, don't start that again."

Maude stares at the telephone dial. If the girl sent for her, she would go, and Nalia could do what she wants, burn the house down for all she cares.

She puts down the phone and bustles to the gate, unhooks the padlock. These days, she just hooks it through the chain without clicking it shut. What was the use of all that locking and unlocking anyway? That stranger just came and cut it open in a minute when he wanted to. He wasn't a bad man, she thinks now. She would have thought so then, too, but she has been too stupid herself, believing everything Nalia told her, right from the start. How else could she have known what to think? When she came to work here, she was younger than the girl is now. Sixteen, a raw Coloured girl from the country. So how could she know?

"Ma'am?"

"Close and lock the garage, please," Nalia says, walking down to the gate.

As soon as the girl returns, she will go inland again, she decides. She misses the dust in her nostrils, and then the mountains, blue in the distance, the night in the little hotel, and the pleasure of the long drive home. There is a whole notebook of things now that she intends to read to Katzenbogen. They will sit in his little room, drinking his strong coffee, and she will read, and he will listen. And then, when he comes to her at the hotel, he will lie there, that sorry figure of a man, stretched out naked on the bed, like a dead rabbit, and he will tell her what he thinks.

The table has been laid for two, Nalia requires that at every meal. Maude must also cook for two, and change the flowers every morning, bake twice a week. Once Maude would have been waiting for the girl just like Nalia, lighting a candle for her every night. But lately Maude has been thinking only of her own future. She is impatient for it, desperate as she stands there waiting for Nalia to finish her pickled fish.

"Ma'am?"

"What?"

"Something I got to tell you, ma'am."

Nalia puts down her knife and fork. She should have sacked Maude with all the others, but she was weak — a weak and stupid old woman who can't fend for herself, even after everything she has endured. "Cough it up," she says. "What is it?"

Maude backs away to the door. "The girl is having a baby. Her father said I must tell you."

Nalia cocks her head, she twists slowly in her chair to look at Maude. "So why doesn't he tell me himself?"

Maude knows the answer to this: He is a coward and a thief and a snake in the grass. She knows that Nalia is right, she has always been right even though she is a madwoman. But any minute she is going to throw that glass, or tear open her dress and all the buttons will go flying. One Friday afternoon, when Maude came home from school to say the girl wasn't waiting at the gate as usual, Nalia threw a pot of face cream at her, but it hit the mirror instead and cracked it. Maude herself had to phone the Mother Superior to find out where the girl was. And, after all, it was only detention for cheekiness. Seven years of bad luck for nothing.

Nalia pushes her chair back and stands, steadying herself on the table. Then she closes her eyes for that dense moment of silence that she has always needed before going onstage. What has her life been if not a string of such moments, half dead, half alive? Had she not withstood the nonentity all these years — ah, what would she be then? Lower than the lowest of captives. She would be sweeping the floor for his leavings. She would be nothing herself.

"I shall wait," she says, sighing into the receiver. "Tell him I shall wait as long as he keeps me waiting."

She keeps her back to Maude, staring out into the garden. They were out in his launch the day he gave her the deed to the house, beyond the bay, out in the open sea. He looked like Neptune up there at the wheel, with his hair blown back in ringlets. When he pointed out the house to her, high up on the hill, she couldn't find it from so far away. "There," he said, "*there!* Can't you *see?*" But, the more he tried, the more she laughed. She almost let the wind blow the deed itself out of her hand, laughing in terror at the thought that, for the first time since the War, she wished to take a step into the future. That she was happy.

"Yes, Maude has told me," Nalia says. "When? Where?"

Maude watches from the door. Usually, people who have suffered dry up like wood, but Nalia has a young woman's skin, younger even than the girl's. The girl is dark and strong like the father, but the mother is light and smooth. When Maude first came for the job, it was the skin she noticed first, and then the voice, and then the way Nalia laughed at all the wrong things.

And then suddenly, Nalia is folding, she is falling to the floor, taking the phone down with her.

"Ma'am!" Maude runs to her. She kneels next to her and cups her hand around Nalia's jaw. *"Madam!"*

Nalia's eyelids flutter.

"Wake up!" Maude shouts. "We can take a ship and go to her! Ma'am, wake up!"

But Nalia wants only to sleep now. She can hear Maude, and the lawn mower, and the nonentity's voice calling through the receiver. She can hear them although she is sleeping so deeply that nothing, not even a fire, could rouse her. When Maude calls out to her, it is like pain, it is like death. She tries to say this, but she is too heavy to utter the words, too heavy even to lift her hand. Down here, she has all the peace she has ever wanted, lovely and thick and deep. She never wants it to end.

8

My husband is my father's cousin. More than this, I look just like his mother, he says. Everything about me reminds him of her, even the way I cry for what I have left behind. His mother begged to be sent back to her own country, but his father said it was impossible. After his father died, my husband made plans to take her there himself. He petitioned the government, paid large sums of money. But then, just as they were about to leave, she died, too. He has tears in his eyes when he tells me this.

I ask to see a photograph of her, and he brings out a faded snapshot of a young girl in a white dress, sitting on a rock wall. She is not beautiful at all. She is serious and plain, with a long nose like mine, and wide dark eyes in a flat face. I go to stand in front of the mirror to see myself as he sees me. But all I see there is what I know too well already. Am I plain, or am I beautiful? I do not know anymore.

He never gives me warning when he is going away. He just goes, and I am still too proud to ask him to stay with me. Every time he comes home, he brings me presents though — a beaver coat with a hat to match, and a diamond bangle, and this beautiful notepaper with my own name at the top. He has never asked me to take his name for the simple reason that I don't know what it is. Nor have I asked him. What would be the point? He only tells me things when he wants me to know them. And so it has become a pattern between us: I never ask, I never thank him, either.

I like him best when he comes home from his shipyard on the mainland. The shipyard is hot, he says, and foul, and smoky. As soon as he is home, he runs his bath full of the hottest water and then steps into it as if it is nothing. The bath is massive, like him, deep and wide and made of dark grey marble. I like to sit cross-legged on the ledge at the back just to watch him under the water.

"Coming in?" He has one gold tooth that flashes when he smiles. I am never prepared for it, and then there it is, gleaming. He reaches for my feet and pulls them into the water, slides his fingers between my toes. He has a gold ring on his little finger that I like to see there, and his palms are pink from the heat of the water. He runs his hands up my legs, wetting them, warming them. "My Paradise," he says. "My Queen."

His rooms are above mine, but farther along the cliff. They are built out into a tower, with windows all around, and no terrace to walk out onto. When I hear the water running up there, I unlock my door to the stairs and climb softly, barefoot, round and round on the cold stone. It is a game I like to play, waiting on the landing to see if I can surprise him. But I never can. He can smell me, he says, he can feel the air move with my breath.

I lean back against the wall of the bath and close my eyes. Every moment of happiness only carries me back to the thought of you, Ma. It is a sickness, this longing for you, it is like death. I try to remind myself of the times I hated you, the leap in my blood when you would fasten your anger on me. And all those names you would call me — thief! tart! trollop!

When I threw them back at you that once, when I screamed, "You are an ugly tart! You are Katzenbogen's tart!" you just stopped and stared at me, your eyes as big as I have ever seen them. And that's when I knew — in that little silence before you leapt and dug your nails into the flesh of my arms, before I locked my own fingers around the roots of your hair — that is when I knew that I was right.

"Go and live with *him!*" I screamed. "I won't be your whole family! I *refuse* to be your whole family!"

You let go of my arms then. You even stood back and smiled, a frightening, cold, triumphant smile. "Ha!" you said, "that's one thing you can never refuse, my dear."

My tears were streaming, I wanted to punish you for Katzenbogen, for the whole long boring War that you shared every week.

"I'm going to live with my father!" I shouted. I turned to leave, to go to the phone and tell him to send me the driver, or the police, or anything. You could follow me all you liked, I'd never come back again, I'd never even look at you again.

And then I turned just to see if you were following, and there you were, sinking against the rocking chair like a pile of old washing. "Ma!" I ran up. But you were folding yourself down onto the floor like the Indian woman on the corner who pretends to be crippled.

You were acting, I could see that you were acting. "Ma!" I said again, stamping my foot. I wanted to kick you, I wanted to make you stop.

But you just winced and turned your head away as if I had really kicked you. And, oh, I despised you then! I hated you with all my heart. And even so, I was waiting, I was longing for you to look up at me so that I could tell you the truth. That I would never leave you, not for my father, not for anyone on earth. Never, never, never.

I stare at my husband, rising from the bath. "I want to go home," I say.

He smiles at me, rubbing himself dry with the towel. It is a smile I have seen him use on the cabin steward and on the sisters who work here. It isn't a smile at all really, it is a reminder that things are not as he expects them to be. Until now, he has never used it on me.

"Just for a holiday," I say. I hear the wheedle in my voice and I despise it. So I clear my throat and start again. "I want to go home to see my mother," I say. "I want to have my baby there."

He reaches out and tries to catch me, to wrap me up with him in his towel. He often does this, and I like it. It is warm in there, and damp and lovely.

This time, however, I jump out of the way. I run down the stairs, down to my room, and slam and bolt the doors. Then I sit on my bed and stare at the cold window, full of pity for myself. I am a freak of nature, Ma, with no friend but you, and a husband before I have even had a boyfriend. I try to cry at all of this, but I am only listening for his step outside the door, wanting him to beg me to come out.

If I were home, you would leave me there to cook. You would make sure that I heard you laughing downstairs with Maude, or playing the piano, or singing. Then you'd call me down for supper as if nothing had happened, and, if I didn't appear, you would send Maude up with a tray. "Knock knock," Maude would say, coming in anyway.

"It is almost spring," my husband shouts through the door. "There will be wildflowers all over the mountain, you'll see how beautiful it is here."

I shake my head. "You're a liar!" I say. "You lie about every single thing."

I can hear him sigh, his slippers shuffling on the stone floor. The truth is childish to him, girlish and boring and dangerous. He waves a hand at it as if he's chasing a fly.

"What do you want to know?" he says. "I will tell you if I can."

I jump off the bed and go to stand at the door. If I could bear to see his face, I would open it, I would watch his eyes as he spoke. "I want to know why you chose me," I say.

He is silent for some moments, so that I think he has crept away. But then he says, "I had a wager with your father, a sort of joke. We have a history of such jokes between us. Women mostly, harmless stuff."

The words fall through the air like stones.

"With this one, I demanded his favourite daughter as payment. And he demanded marriage in exchange. I remember laughing, because marriage was another joke between us. We were a little high on cognac, but I agreed."

I can hardly breathe under the weight of his words. All my life I have known how to hate a man, but now it is as if I know nothing.

"Then he took me to the City Hall to see you. You were six or seven at the time, sitting in the front row, watching your mother sing. He had given you a box of chocolates. 'Look,' he said, 'she won't dare to open it.' And you didn't. You sat there through the whole performance with those chocolates on your lap. I wanted to save you right then, but I decided to wait."

In one movement I slide the bolt and open the door. He is black in the fading light. All I can see are his eyes and his teeth, and if I had a knife, I would stab him.

He takes a step forward, but I hold up my hand and he stops.

"*Save me?*" I shout.

"What intrigued me," he says quickly, "and for all the years that followed, was the thought of that child, my cousin's child — of you, as my wife. And then, just when I was growing a bit tired of the idea, your father arranged for me to see you again. Fate has an odd way with jokes, doesn't it?"

I stare at him as if I am waiting for more. But the words have been said now, and they only make me think of you putting on your blue silk for him, and your black evening pearls, and then going down to him without me, thinking only of yourself.

"You are a *joke!*" I shout at him. "You are *old* and ugly and I cannot stand the sight of you!"

"I know, I know."

"You *don't* know! *What* do you know?" I run to the window so that he won't see me sobbing.

He follows me, he folds his arms around me at last.

"*She* is my Queen!" I sob. "*She* is my Paradise!"

"I know," he says. He kisses my neck, my hair. "But please, Thea, please don't ask me to send you back to her now."

❧ 9 ❧

It is Braughton who has suggested that Nalia lock up the house and go inland for a spell. The old Leyfield mansion has been converted into a retreat for musicians, he says. There are pianos up there, and concerts, and lovely walks in the hills. She could do with a rest after what she's been through, why not give it a try?

She waves him off. A rest from what? From punishment? Katzenbogen says she must have wanted the girl to be taken away, why else would she have invited the Syrian in? But what does he know about vanity, that old fool? Nalia has burned the blue silk to ashes in the servants' incinerator. She has thrown away her makeup too, and let her hair go grey. When it is long enough, she will wear it in a bun, like her grandmother. The old woman is back in Nalia's dreams now, but young again, with her bony patrician face and Titian hair. And yet she is confused with the girl herself, with Nalia, too. Every night, Nalia expects a visit from all three.

As a girl herself, Nalia had loved that old woman immoderately. In the summer, when they went to the cottage, she would watch her undo her long grey hair and swim naked, right out to the middle of the lake. Every morning, when she went onto the lawn before breakfast to do her calisthenics, Nalia went too. The old woman had breasts like sea shells, a round stomach, and flat, pale buttocks that Nalia loved to look at. Once, her grandmother found a lover up at the lake, a common working-man, much younger than herself. He would come and knock at the back door, and off she would go with him, into the woods.

Nalia rings the bell for Maude. "Get my suitcases down, please."

"Where you going?"

"None of your business. Do as you are told."

When Maude comes back with the suitcases, she finds Nalia wrapping and folding all the wrong way, the clothes scattered and piled around the room. She picks them up and puts them on the divan. She has cleaned them all herself, pressed them, lifted the hems and let them down again. She begins to pack with quick, deft movements. "Why no evening shoes for the black dress?" she asks, fetching them from the wardrobe. She picks up a nightie and holds it to the light. "The moths got this old thing," she says, "we must chuck it away."

Nalia walks out onto the verandah. If she were to take Maude with her, she would use her like a fan, like a mask. The other musicians there won't have servants, they'll be living on charity. Braughton has suggested that she might consider making a donation herself, and she thinks that she might, although she can ill afford it. Not even Braughton knows how her money has dwindled over the years, how she has to make do.

"What about jewelry?" Maude says.

"I won't need it."

"Where you going then?"

Nalia leans over the parapet. The evening is lovely, soft and warm, the hot season must be on its way in early. One of these days, she should consider going north, back to her own mountains, or even to the lake. She could take Maude with her, have her drape the house just as they draped and locked the cottage for the winter. Now that the girl is gone, Nalia could go anywhere she liked. Egypt — she could go to Egypt. Or to the Baltic, like her grandmother. Her heart lifts at the thought of all the freedom she could have, now that the girl is gone.

Without the girl, what is this house anyway? It mocks her and it scolds her. When she sits down to practise, she fiddles with the keys, but there is no life left in the voice. No wonder Braughton wants to send her away for a rest. She's no use to him like this, no use to anyone. She can't even listen to a record anymore. Every bar, every note is unbearably predictable.

So what could Egypt do to change this? If she went, she'd only have to come back again. And the Baltic would be the same. The place to which she really wants to go is possible only in dreams. She wants her grandmother. She wants to follow her down the back stairs and through the kitchen in the early morning chill, with the servants' *maas* fermenting on the stove, and the lake still covered in mist.

It was her own mother who had tried to separate her from her grandmother right from the beginning. The old woman was wild, she said, not to be trusted with children. Once, her grandmother had caught Nalia's father in his study, sprawled over the maid, and after that, she had called him The Sprawler. If he scowled, he was The Scowler. He was also The Sulker and

The Shouter and The Fool. But mostly he was The Sprawler, which amused her best. Nalia's mother warned guests about her mother at the front door. She was not to be trusted, they were told. They were not to believe a word she said.

"Ma'am —" Maude is standing in the doorway, holding the large cake tin. "Here are all the letters from the girl."

Nalia turns to face her. How old would Maude be now? Thirty-five? Thirty-six? There's the odd grey hair, and her nose has broadened a bit along with the rest of her. But otherwise she is as she was when she first arrived at the kitchen door all those years ago. At sixteen, she had known just what she wanted — a room inside the house, not in the servants' quarters, and Sundays off to go to Mass. Nalia liked that. And she liked the cold black eyes, the severe shelf of bosom. Better than a husband, Nalia thought, better than a common servant, too.

And she was right. Maude was apt, she was quick, and, best of all, she understood loss and punishment. It was she who had suggested the convent for the girl. It would keep her away from the riffraff and common rubbish, she said. Her own mother had thrown her out to find a job in town. She had been the cleverest girl in the mission school, the nuns wanting her for themselves, but still her mother had said, Rubbish, time to find a job.

"Bring them to me in the lounge after supper," Nalia says. Now that she is going away, she thinks that she can bear the thought of the girl again. Perhaps she can even bear to know where she is, what has happened.

When Maude brings the cake tin in with the coffee tray, Nalia is waiting on the couch. "You can go now," she says.

But Maude does not leave. The letters have been coming for months now, sometimes two or three at once. When Nalia leaves them on the kist unopened, it is Maude who takes them away and hides them at the back of the pantry.

"Read them from this end," she says, "this one's the first." She wants a chance to stay and read them herself. She wants to ask Nalia's forgiveness for phoning the girl's father, too. But that is impossible. Everyone knows you can never say sorry to Nalia. It only reminds her of everything there is to be sorry about.

Nalia pulls out a letter from the middle. "Bring me the letter opener, please."

And so Maude fetches it for her. She sits on the floor next to the couch, picking up the envelopes and the pages that Nalia throws down. Sometimes, Nalia just closes her eyes and breathes. Sometimes, she bursts forth with a roar, and then she will keep that page for herself, reading it to Maude first. "Just listen to this —" she'll say.

The grandfather clock rolls through its ten o'clock chimes and Maude begins to gather up the pages Nalia has dropped. "Ma'am," she says, "it is late."

"Leave them where they are," Nalia says.

"But the dogs will chew them."

Nalia glares at her. "Then take the dogs and lock them in the kitchen. If any letters are chewed, it will be your fault."

When Maude has left, Nalia takes off her glasses and holds the pages to her face to breathe them in. Did she want the girl punished that badly? Everyone punished? Even herself? Yes, yes she did. There was to be no bottom to the punishment her own silence was to achieve. She picks up a page and examines the date. 15 February. And another, March. April. July. She snatches up an envelope. Yes, a local postmark. So they come through the nonentity after all, and, if she writes back, it must go through him, too. Soon, the child will be born, and even then, the nonentity is the one who will have to tell her.

Nalia sinks back onto the cushions. How can any treachery she has known compare to this? Week after week during those months at the slimming salon, she might have seen it coming. She had watched the girl adoring herself in the mirror — the flat, muscled stomach, the breasts and the legs and the skin. She had listened to her diaries, too, but what had she heard?

Between love and hate, there is only circumstance, Nalia knows this. Once, she followed her grandmother to the tram, onto the tram and into town. When the old woman got off, Nalia did, too. She hung back, she followed, she watched her grandmother go into the chemist, the patisserie, the library. Nalia could easily have gone with her if she had asked. She often went to town with her grandmother. But what she wanted this time was to catch the old woman out — with a secret, a secret person closer to her heart than she. She wanted to hate the old woman, even for a day. And then, all through supper that night, she found that she hated her anyway. It was as if, indeed, the old woman had betrayed her. It was almost like pleasure, that hatred high in her throat. And it was every bit as strong as love.

Part Two

My husband's name is Naim. This I find out the day my twins are born. All through my confinement, I have cried out for him, but, without his name, the doctor has not understood what I wanted. And then, once it is over and the babies are carried off, in he comes at last, bringing with him the smell of the outside world — tobacco and leather and Paco Rabane.

"The wildflowers have come out for you," he says. "They are dancing all over the mountain." His fingernails are manicured and the gold ring gleams.

But for three days, a woman has been sitting in the shadows. She is tall and beaky like a stork, and she crochets without dropping her eyes from me. She has brought a small grey monkey, which runs up the curtains and along the rods. When I tried to tear the bandages from my breasts and the woman rose clucking and scolding, the monkey came down scolding, too, right onto the bed.

"Who *is* she?" I shout at my husband. "Where has she taken my babies?"

He sits on the bed and takes my hand, but I pull it back.

"What have you done with them?" I cry.

He doesn't answer. For all I know, he could have thrown them down the cliff, or put them out on the mountain for the wolves. He calls the woman, and she comes to stand at the bed, dark and solid and unsmiling.

"This is Sonja," he says. "She is my half-sister."

"I don't *care* who she is!" I shout. "I don't *want* her here!"

"The children are fine, Thea," he says, "they are sleeping."

His voice lulls me, and I try to believe him. But the first girl was born with a harelip, and the second was covered in dark, silky hair like an animal. When I cried out at the sight of them, they all laughed. And then the nurses took them away, leaving only this woman to spy on me.

"Come," he says, "let me take you out onto the terrace to see the flowers."

I let him lift me and stand me up like an invalid, lead me outside to stand at the railing.

"Just look," he says, "everywhere you can see. They have come out for you; the wrong time of the year completely."

He is right, there are flowers all down the mountain, yellow and blue and red. They toss and bend under a strong breeze off the sea. But they have not come out for me. They are his flowers. They are his birds, too — his scrub, his wind, his sea. He points to these flowers and those flowers, telling me their names. But at home, we had our own names for what was all around us — frangipani, jacaranda, mango and gula-gula, kikuyu, hadedah, shongololo. I use the words now only because I am writing them down. And yet they are not really names at all — they are the place itself. They are what held us together in that place, my mother and me.

He reaches into the pocket of his cardigan and pulls out a telegram. "This came for you this morning," he says.

I stare at it for a moment as if it were a trick. Then I snatch it from him, I tear it in my haste to open the envelope, and have to hold it together up to the sunlight to read. Six words dance there without meaning until I can slow my breathing and read them one by one.

BRING THE BABIES HOME STOP MA

So this is the way it happens. Just as you forget what you have been longing for, in it slips like a thief. And yet I had not forgotten; I had been remembering my other life as if I no longer had any claim on it, as if remembering itself had become my enemy. And now here she is in my hand. Her furious voice, her furious demands.

"Thea —" He rests his elbows on the railing and looks out to sea. "You have never asked me for my name."

I fold my arms against the wind, hugging the telegram to my chest. Natalia and Theadora, Nalia and Thea.

"Naim," he says. "My name is Naim."

I stare at him, this stranger who has never had a name. Ever since that first day on the sleeping porch, I have been waiting for him. I have listened for his footstep, for the sound of his car, for his bathwater running. But I have never needed his name. And now I have it. Naim. It is lovely after all, like the cries of the gulls circling above us. I will think of him as a gull, I decide. I will think of him as an enormous, dark, dangerous gull, whose prisoner I am now more surely than ever.

❧ 2 ❧

Nalia never attends the afternoon performances in the hotel lounge. She has a waiter bring her tea down to the cottage, all her other meals as well. "Amateurs and has-beens," she grumbles to Maude, "let them entertain each other."

"Maybe it would be nice to go up there just once," Maude suggests. She has heard what the others say about Nalia. They say she is a has-been herself, that the daughter ran off like a chorus girl, and who could blame her? The mother is mad, they say, she's always been mad, for all her fame and fortune.

Nalia sits on the verandah steps with her cup and saucer. She loves the smell of the thatch heated by the afternoon sun. She loves the smell of everything — floor polish, fireplace, coir matting. The cottage seems to hold the whole mountain range to itself. It is as if — with her sitting there, holding her tea, smelling the thatch — as if the world is empty of everything but this moment.

When they first arrived, the manager led her to a suite in the main hotel, two interleading rooms with a small bathroom off the bedroom.

"But where is my maid to sleep?" Nalia asked, looking around at the faded old florals and wicker. "Where is her bathroom?"

"There's a room in the staff quarters for her," he said. "She'll have to share, of course. They all have to share."

Nalia raised her chin at him. "You will kindly move a bed in here for her," she said.

"Sorry, madam," he said, staring down at his shoes, "that's not possible. What would the others say?"

Nalia has never bothered to answer such questions. "Maude," she said, "put our things back in the car immediately."

"No, just wait a minute, madam," said the manager. "Just let me go up to the office and telephone Mr. James."

Nalia waited. She had sent a handsome cheque to this Mr. James ahead of time with just such a scene in mind. And she'd had a handsome letter of thanks from him in response.

When the manager returned, he was smiling. "If you would follow me," he said, leading them away from the hotel, down past the tennis courts, to a little thatched cottage with its own walled garden. "This is where Mr. James stays when he comes up. He says you're welcome to stay here, both of you."

And so, for six weeks now, Nalia has been happy here. The cottage is just what she could have wished for — two bedrooms en suite, with a sitting room between them, a baby grand, roses in the garden, and the amphitheatre of mountains around them.

Except for Maude and her warbling, her candles burning every night under thatch ready to go up like a haystack, the arrangement is perfect. Nalia has to hand it to Braughton. Living in three rooms away from her old life has returned some of her hope. Why hadn't she thought of this for herself? She loves to hear the baboons barking, to have the air washed clean by the afternoon thunderstorms. For half a day at a time, she can even forget that the girl is gone, that she has had not one baby, but two, and that those children will be closer to her than Nalia herself has ever been.

Katzenbogen would be the first to point out that this is normal, this is life. But Nalia doesn't give a damn about normal life. Every morning, she wakes out of the same nightmare. The girl is home — she is at the airport, looking for her luggage. But when Nalia shouts from the other side of the barrier, she doesn't hear her. When she turns in Nalia's direction, she doesn't see her either.

Nalia startles awake, staring up into the dark vortex of the thatch while her heart slows its thudding. For three weeks now, she has been waking out of this dream to the same mystery. If it is only a dream, why do I still want her punished?

But then, by the time she is out on the lawn, preparing for her calisthenics, the nightmare is forgotten and she is a girl again herself. With the sun not yet risen, the mountains are blue-grey and mysterious like the mountains of the lake. If she closes her eyes, there really could be a lake out there, and the lovely smell of pine, frost on the grass under her feet. She lifts her chin and takes a deep breath. After all these years, her body remembers every position as if there were music behind it. She can even feel her grandmother's hand on her shoulder. "Good, Natalia, very good."

As the sun comes over the mountains, the mist lifts like smoke. Her skin is whiter than ever now, and her hair is a short fleece of grey. By the time the sun has risen fully and the mountains are verdant and lush, she has forgotten everything but this extraordinary old happiness. It is the sort of happiness that gives her hope, drawing all sorts of possibilities with it.

Even the African children who come to watch, make her smile. The first week, a few of them gathered on the large flat rock beyond the garden wall and twittered there like birds. When she lifted her face and opened her arms, the biggest boy, a showoff, stood up and copied her. She laughed and they all laughed back. So now, there are more than a dozen waiting for her every morning. Once a week, she walks down the road to the supply store to buy them sweets. And then, every Friday, they gather at the garden gate, almost naked themselves, with their hands cupped, waiting.

"You should cover yourself to give them the sweets," Maude grumbles. "Hamba!" she shouts, storming the wall like a rhinoceros. And they scatter, waiting at a distance, laughing at her too.

"Who asked you?" says Nalia. She calls the children back.

Maude clicks her tongue. She is tired of being nanny to this old woman. Are they going to live here forever, in these three rooms? And the waiters after her every day with their cheeky remarks? On the first Sunday, Nalia drove her to find the mission church beyond the village, but the roads were muddy from the rain and they didn't have chains. So now there are only walks to the supply store, and walks up the mountain before lunch, and Maude is completely sick of it.

And then, one day, a man comes out of the mist like a ghost himself. When he sees Nalia on the lawn, he stops, but she has her eyes closed to the sun rising over the mountain. He is wearing shorts and a leather hat, and he smiles as he watches this pale, slim, old woman dancing in the cold morning air. He puts his pipe between his teeth, bends to light it.

Nalia smells the tobacco, but she doesn't stop to look. She twists and bends, straightens, twists and bends the other way. Somehow, over the weeks, she has known that someone would come for her here. She has known this without even knowing that she knew it. Nor did she know that it would be a man. She just knew that something would sniff out her happiness, would come up here and fall into the trap of it.

And so she is unsurprised when she sees him on the garden wall, lounging there impudently, a shadow against the sun. When she has finished her exercises, she shades her eyes and frowns at him. He is dark from the sun, and dusty — a farmer or a cattleman or someone's indolent husband. But it is a long time since she has been looked at the way he is looking at her now, and so she breathes it in, she lifts her chin as if she were about to sing.

"Hey, that's good," he says. The voice is dark like him, thick and dry and badly used.

"Here, ma'am —" Maude brings her dressing gown, and holds it open for her. "The breakfast is coming," she says. "Better get dressed."

But Nalia walks over to the garden wall. "What do you want?" she says to the man.

He laughs as if he is used to such questions from naked women. "Just looking," he says. "No harm in looking, hey?"

She turns back to the cottage. With every step she is more sure that he will wait for her. And so she takes her time. When she comes out again, dressed in her walking skirt and carrying her stick, he stands up, unsure. But she opens the gate and starts down the path to the river, so he follows, just as she knows he will. When she stops at the crossing, judging the water, he comes up behind her. "Here," he says, "this is the way."

She watches him dance across from rock to rock, wetting his dusty boots. He is a dancer, she decides, he is a ghost and a dancer, sent here to delight her. He runs back across the stones to take her hand, and she gives it to him, letting him lead her across.

On the other side, he turns upriver, walking ahead, stopping, turning, coming back for her like a dog. She has never noticed this path before. It is damp and noisy with the river roaring past, and no one would ever hear if she shouted. But if he is a murderer, she is quite ready, just as she is when she lets the car fly down hill after hill, coming back from Katzenbogen. Katzenbogen says that it is another way of punishing everyone, this readiness for death. But he is wrong, as usual. If she is ready to die, it is only because she cannot bear to wait.

They follow the river for about a mile before he turns into the hill and climbs. They are near the gorge now, she can hear the waterfall roaring. Perhaps that is how he will do it, then — throw her into the heart of it. She stops to look back at the hotel. It is always lovely to see it from above — the thatch, the lawns and gardens and ponds and pools, all gleaming in the morning sun.

"Come," he says, holding out a hand again.

But she plants her walking stick. She has come far enough, and she is tiring of the game.

"Just over there," he says, pointing to a dark slash in the hillside.

She sniffs the air, as if she can smell it at this distance, damp and foul. "Baboons live in caves," she says.

"Then we won't go there. *Please!*"

How does he know how to ask her like this? Not to smile, but to beg, to long, to need. He must be half baboon himself, she decides. She follows him into the shade of the cliff and stands there quite still as he unbuttons her walking skirt.

He doesn't try to kiss her, just grasps her to him, his body urgent and furious. She listens to his breathing, stares at his hat, floating beside her face. It smells of sweat and tobacco, of dust and bad food. From now on, she decides, it will be the smell of his need, this lovely raw need so long absent from her life. And yet so familiar too — so perfectly, perfectly foreseen.

🐝 3 🐝

Even the children are in his shadow, Ma. The nurses circle them with their harsh voices so that I can't hear them at all. When I fall asleep, they vanish into dreams. And then, when I wake up, it is as if they had never burned themselves through me. And yet I know that they are mine as surely as I am yours. They are mine and they are yours. They are ours together.

Every morning and afternoon, the nurses take them out for a walk, and I follow at a distance like a ghost. I watch them lay a rug out under the trees, and give the babies bottles. They never look at me, but they know that I am there. If I come too close, they pack the babies up and move away. And so I squat where I am, in the shadow of a tree, silent, watching like a thief.

Sometimes, Sonja comes out to sit with them, and, once they have learned to crawl, the babies go over to her and lift themselves up, reaching for her glasses. She, too, knows that I am there. I can see by the way she lifts them up and holds them so that I can see her thick fingers across their backs and her ugly smile. And then the monkey comes flying out of the trees, baring its teeth, and she hands the baby back to the nurses.

You would shout at me for this too, Ma. You would say, What's the matter with you? Send that creature away! But when I shout at Naim about her, he just shrugs, as if there is nothing he can do. The children don't interest him, nor does the fighting of women. What he has been waiting for all these months, what he is watching for every lunch and every dinner, is for me to stretch my legs out for him again, to lift my hair.

So I hoard myself away from him. I try on the clothes he brings me, but then I put them back in their boxes, folded just the way they came. At dinner, I don't drink the wine he pours for me. If I drank it, I could forget why I want to punish him. I could forget about the children, too, and about Sonja, how I plan to punish her.

All through dinner I watch her, never taking my eyes from her hands as she cuts her meat or lifts it to her mouth. I watch her until she has to lay her knife and fork down and leave the table before pudding is even served.

"Thea," he says when she's gone, "won't you come to me again?" I can smell the wine on his breath as he leans close to me. I am faint with the smell of him, but still I shake my head.

I am thin now, Ma, even thinner than before the babies. Every morning I do the exercises they taught me at the slimming salon, and every night, after my bath, I try on my new clothes. Until now, my favourite has been a summer dress with a jacket to match. It is made in America, and when I put it on, I feel American myself. You would never allow me to wear it. You would say the neckline is too low, and green doesn't go with blue. But it does with this dress. And there's a lovely ruffle of dotted Swiss around the neckline, like a collar. If it were not for Sonja, I would wear it tonight just to see his face. I would put on my pearls too, and let my hair loose.

But Sonja is always there. She is the one he sends to deliver the new clothes to my room. I listen for her heavy tread down the passage, her keys clinking in her pocket. She has keys to every room in the villa, even to Naim's study. I have seen her go in there when he is away, and bolt the door, staying as long as she likes.

Even when there is no box to deliver, she goes into my room. I can smell her monkey in there, and once she forgot to close the drawer of my desk. So I hide my notebooks in the back of my wardrobe, and today I am hiding there myself, with the door slightly ajar. I know she will come this afternoon. Naim has come home. I have heard him calling to the sisters to bring in his luggage.

When she does come, she knocks only once, and then in she comes, and the monkey is up the curtain as usual. She thinks I am outside, watching the children. I followed them out there as usual, but then, when I heard the funicular start up, I crept back and came to hide in the wardrobe.

The monkey knows I am here. He is screeching at her about it. But she has placed the box on my bed and is opening it quickly, folding back the tissue and lifting out a dress. It is a beautiful dress, old-fashioned and modern at the same time, with a fitted bodice, right up to the chin, and a slight train behind. She carries it to the mirror and stands there with it clasped to her throat.

I watch her wanting it for herself, and I am frozen with hard pleasure. The dress is mine, the children are mine as well. They are more mine than anyone else's, even Naim's. One day, I will tell them this. I will find a way to rip them from his eyes. But, for now, I must wait. Even you would have to wait, Ma, just as you waited through the War. You would have to hide here as I am, watching your husband's sister hold your dress up to her chin and begin to cry — blotching the beautiful silk all down the front with her tears.

"Stop it!" I shout, jumping out of the wardrobe and grabbing the dress from her. "You are spoiling my dress! I'll call Naim! Naim! NAIM!" I shout.

She wheels on me then and claps her hand over my mouth, almost stopping my breathing. She would kill me if she could, I know she would, so I bite her hand hard and she jumps back with a cry.

"Ugly!" I shout at her. "You are old and ugly and you will *never* have my children!"

But she has run out of the room and down the passage, the keys clanking wildly, and the monkey screaming behind her.

When I arrive at the dining room that evening, Naim takes in everything at once — the dress, the lipstick, my hair loose around my shoulders. He doesn't smile, he just says, "Who's for champagne tonight? Sonja? Champagne?"

She shakes her head, pretending to examine a stain on the tablecloth. But her ears are red and her face is pale, and I don't need to ask myself how a sister or even a half sister could be jealous of her brother's wife. With jealousy, there is no asking why. She is ugly and she is jealous, and there is nothing I could do to help her, even if I wanted to.

The dress moves around me like water as I walk to my place. When I look across at Sonja and smile, Naim smiles, too. He opens the champagne and pours us each a glass, and we drink and eat and talk as if Sonja were not there at all. From now on, I decide, I will wear a new dress every evening. And when I go to his study, I will be sure that she sees me going, that she hears him slide the bolt behind me. If he has brought her here to be mother to my children and jailer to me, still, every day, she will know that he is my real jailer, that she is nothing to me, or to my children either.

The next morning, I go out to meet them. It is spring again in the garden, warm and fragrant, even humid under the trees. On the other side of the villa, the sun flames down so strongly that I cannot stand out on my terrace any more. Every window is closed against it, every curtain drawn. But here, in the front, the windows are open, there is Mozart playing, the rabbits are out. The children crawl after them, and they disappear into the trees like ghosts.

I have decided to give the children names. Their real names are long and ugly, and I don't want to learn them. So I call them Mina and Nema. Mina is Naim's name turned inside out. And Nema is named for no one. You would scold me for this, Ma. You would tell me I'm being too clever by half. But Naim doesn't even notice them, he doesn't care.

Mina and Nema, Nema and Mina — I sing the names to myself like a lullaby, strolling up to Mina and standing at a safe distance. She sits back and frowns up at me. The hair on her body has fallen out now, just as Naim said it would. He himself was born covered in hair, he has told me. When it fell out, they gathered it and put it in a small gold box, as hers has been, too. She looks like his mother, he says, she looks like me too. So I stare at her the way I stared at that photograph of the girl on the wall, but all I see is the ape child they first held up to me — a wild thing, a stranger just like him.

"I am your mother," I whisper. I give a laugh in case she begins to scream. But she doesn't, she just looks up at me and cocks her head. So I do it again, and this time she smiles. She looks like the child of a Gypsy. There are four gleaming teeth now, and little gold hoops threaded through her ears, a tiny ring on her finger, and a miniature bangle on each wrist — gold and amethyst and pearl.

"Thea!" Naim is at the study window.

I take her hands and dance with her. "Gypsy child, Gypsy child, Mina, Mina, Mina," I lift her and fold her into my arms. She is soft, and brown from the sun, and she smells of sour milk and the bitter island soap they all use. Everything here smells of that soap.

"Thea!"

But I am drunk with the smell of her now, mad with this sudden happiness. I kiss her neck, her hair. I stroke the soft flesh of her thighs. "I am your mother," I sing, "your mother, your mother, your mother."

When I put her down at last, she cries out, and I turn, remembering how I cried myself up on the sleeping porch, watching you pick your way along the crazy paving to the garage. You never turned when I banged on the window, never. And when you had gone, Maude would come up to find me. "What's the good of crying for nothing?" she would say. "She's coming back tomorrow. Time to grow up now."

* * *

When I arrive at his study door, he does not come to embrace me as usual. "I have something to ask you," he says.

I stand still as a pillar. I cannot bear him to ask for things from me. I want him to take what he wants as if I have no choice.

"I am going away tomorrow," he says. "It would please me greatly if you would leave the children to Sonja."

"*Sonja?*" I shout as if he were deaf.

He comes over to me then and lays his hands on my shoulders, but I shrug them off. I don't want him to touch me. I want a normal husband, I want to be a normal mother too.

"I want to go home!" I shout. "I want to show my babies to my mother!" I do want this. But what I really long for is the life that other girls have — 'varsity and boyfriends and learning to drive — even though it is too late, even though it has always been too late.

"Thea," he says, "your mother has gone away. The house has been locked up for some months."

I stare at him, but he is only a dark shape now, immense and solid against the windows. If I were a normal girl, would I know what I was seeing, Ma? Even when I try to look at him through your eyes, all I see is you at the top of the table in your blue silk, like a ghost, and him waiting for his chance to catch my eye. And yet, when he is gone, I will be waiting for him to come back. I will be listening for the gate again, watching the dogs for signs.

"You're a liar," I say, laughing hard and cold. "You're the *King* of Liars!"

"As you like." He goes to the window to look out again. He is used to my insults by now, he is bored with them. "She has gone to the mountains," he says. "She is in fine health."

I sink against the back of the chair. You have always told me that you can tell a liar by his eyes. I do not need to see his eyes to hear the truth of the words themselves. You have gone to the mountains and locked up the house. You have left me, Ma, and I have nowhere to go home to now, even if I could.

"Come," he says, "come with me." He takes my hand and leads me like a child to the divan. I let him lay me back there and close my eyes with his fingertips, trace my eyebrows, my cheeks, my jaw, my neck. It is as if he is a blind man trying to know what he cannot see. His touch is so light that it is almost nothing, and yet it stops all my questions as he knows it will. It stops everything but the knowledge that I am living two lives, the one in which I know what I think and what I want, and the other this — his hands at my waist, on my hips, lifting me like a cup, like a bowl, so that I am nothing without him to use me like this, and I will never be free.

❦ 4 ❦

Maude has never been able to stand scales — every afternoon, up and up, and then down and down. She picks up her knitting bag and goes out, down the path to the thatched shelter next to the tennis courts. No one plays tennis in this place, they're too old, so she comes here whenever she can, and settles into one of the wicker chairs. "Happy days are here again," she hums, taking out her knitting.

She used to sing this to the girl on the way home from school on Friday afternoons. On Monday mornings, it was "Sentimental Journey." And sometimes, when things were bad, it was "You Are My Lucky Star." When she sings, she remembers everything that has been left behind. "Ai, sooga!" she says to herself, shaking her head.

"Ai, sooga!"

Maude shrinks back into the chair, holding her knitting to her chest like a shield. A man is squatting in the shadow of the wall.

"Don't stop singing, man!" he says, standing up. It is

Sonny, the headwaiter, the cheeky baboon who has been after her from the day they arrived.

"You follow me down here?" she says, her voice shrill. "I'll report you to the manager."

He bares his gums in a parody of terror. "What's wrong with you, hey? I was here first. You followed me, maybe?"

She wraps her knitting around the needles and stabs them into the ball of wool.

"Hey, don't go, man," he says quickly. "Sorry to give you a fright." He is wiry like a monkey, dark skinned too. "It can be lonely here for a chap," he says.

"Where's your wife then?"

"Divorce."

Maude wants to cross herself, but he's watching her, so she pretends to scratch here, scratch there.

"You must be lonely too, hey?" he says.

"Not lonely, no." But it is a lie. Maude is lonely to the bottom of her heart. It is the way she was lonely when she came to work for Nalia in the first place. Every night, she covered her face with her towel and sobbed, in an ecstasy of misery. But she was young then, she was lonely for her hopes and dreams. Now she is lonely for the life she has made for herself with Nalia and the girl, all the habits of that life.

He takes a cigarette from behind his ear and lights it. The smell of homemade cigarettes has always pleased Maude, frightened her, too. It is the smell of fathers and brothers, men laughing and making trouble.

"There's a film for us in the back on Saturday nights," he says. "If you like, we can go for a walk on Sunday."

"Ai!" she says, swatting away the suggestion. She opens the

knitting bag and pretends to scramble for something in there. "At home, I go to Mass on Sundays," she says, "with my sister."

"The mission isn't too far to walk."

"We tried to drive. It's too far," she says.

But after church, she and Dorothy walk all the way down to the beach together. They take off their stockings and tuck up their skirts and go down to the water to fill up their bottles. She misses Dorothy, and she misses the sea as well.

"Listen, man," he says, "I'll wait for you on Sunday down by the gate after breakfast. I'll walk with you. Don't let me down, hey?"

Nalia is writing in her notebook when Maude comes in. "I'm going up to dinner tonight," she says without looking up. "I'll wear the black lace." She knows that Maude is sulking. But for now, Nalia won't let one thing spoil the pleasure of her voice coming back, her hope. Perhaps she'll put through a call to Katzenbogen tomorrow, ask him up for a weekend.

What she longs to do is to read him what she has written about the ghost man. How many times has Katzenbogen told her that jealousy has nothing to do with its object? Even the girl's father, he says — even that thief who came in and took the girl away — they only serve to feed the rat already gnawing her insides. She should try to remember as far back as she can go. She should try to go right back to the beginning.

But what can he tell Nalia about memory? Tell me what happened this week as if I am blind and deaf, she used to say to the girl. It was a game she had come up with as a girl herself, lying there, still as death, watching and listening. If she has been jealous of the girl's eyes and ears since she was snatched away, it is because the girl does not know how to use them properly. Everything is in her letters but the thief himself. A ring on a finger? A dark shape under the water, calling her in? What does this tell her? Perhaps the girl doesn't know how to get around the back of that mystery. When she comes home, Nalia will read to her from her own notebook. She will show her how to find the words for a nonentity.

She sips her vodka and looks out over the mountains. Hope brings danger behind it, she knows that. But, sitting there now, smelling the iron on the taffeta, she only wants to think of her voice readying in her lungs, the ghost man waiting for her on the wall every morning. If the girl were to come home tomorrow? Nalia shakes the thought away. Seven months now without a letter, without anything. Why should she even wonder what would happen if the girl were to come home? Or how she had managed when the babies were born?

She herself had been too thin to bleed at the proper time. Bleeding had to wait, like everything else in her life, for the War to be over. And when it was — when she bled at last, and then had the child, and then stopped bleeding completely — it had all seemed to happen in a minute. So what is left now? Her picture all over the papers, someone from the university wanting to write the story of her life? While any common girl in the street can do what she can never do again? What she never wants to do again, either? So where is the loss in all this? Where is the affront?

"Ma'am?" Maude stands ready with the dress. "About the jewels?"

Maude is in love with her jewelry. Perhaps Nalia will leave her the pearl-and-amethyst bracelet in her will. She will drive her to the mission on Sunday for Mass — that will snap her out of this sulk. Nalia herself loves to listen to Africans singing, harmonising like angels. If Maude were an African, she might have a voice worth listening to. But, as it is, the voice is thin as a reed and sharp. Nalia will send her to sit at the other end of the church, and even then she'll probably hear her trilling offkey. If she could, she would forbid Maude to sing at all. She'd also silence the Indian mynahs that nest under the thatch, and Gracie Winthrop, walking past the cottage every day before tea — every *day* that stupid cow turning around to say, "Good after-*nooon* to you, maestra."

Looking at herself in the mirror now, Nalia is sorry that it is not a stage she is walking out onto tonight. The black lace is cut perfectly for her figure — *blouson* on top, fitted around the hips. She has sleeked her hair back behind her ears, and sprayed it there like a Roman helmet. For the first time in a year, she feels ready to perform. She could walk out right now, in fact, with the girl's face in the front row catching the light from the stage, and the nonentity in the loge, thinking she can't see him up there. For eighteen years, he has never missed a performance, and still he thinks she won't look for him, won't see him there behind that pillar.

And yet, standing in front of the mirror, it is not them that she longs for at all. It is that moment when she forgets them, when she forgets herself too. What she longs for now is that moment of silence when it is another future that she has out there before her — a glorious future unable to be stopped.

5

Every morning that Naim is away, I go out to see the children. When I reach down for them now, they hold up their hands and I lift them, I clasp them to me, solid as puppies. They do not understand the fierceness of my pleasure. They struggle, or they laugh as if it is a joke I am playing on them, and I wonder how it would be if they had not been snatched from me. If they were mine as I was my mother's, would I be furious like her? I don't know, I can't even know if she danced with me like this, what pleasure was left to her beyond the triumph of locking my father out.

Sonja is a shadow against a tree. Since Naim went away, she has stopped coming down to my room. Perhaps he told her to leave me alone, now that my mother has left me. Or perhaps she knows that her work was done when I put on the grey silk dress. Whatever the reason, when I come out onto the lawn now, her dark voice stops, and they all turn to watch me.

Today, I have Nema in my arms, sparkling with jewelry. She stares up at me, as usual, waiting for what comes next. "My mother has left me," I sing softly into her hair, "left me, left me, left me." As I begin to dance with her, she winds her fingers around my sundress strap and hangs on as if I might drop her. So I laugh for her as I laughed for Mina. I twirl her around, laughing, until she laughs herself. It is a wild laugh, with her lip pinched up like that — more like a shriek than a laugh — but when I hear it, I stop and clasp her to me tight. I am crying as I kiss her neck, her hair, and I don't care if they are watching, I don't care about anything at all.

Mina crawls up, and holds her arms for me, and cries. And so I lift her, too. They are heavy on my hips, both of them, but as I begin to dance, they lighten, and the laughter becomes a kind of song, a kind of scream among us. We are a three-headed monster howling together, orphaned, homeless, happy.

I come to a stop in the sun, and sink down onto the grass, panting. But they pull at my hair and climb over me, wanting the game to go on. Sonja is watching, she can't help herself watching. She says something to the nurses and they come over to fetch the children.

I close my eyes into the sun as they are carried away. If Sonja were not here to watch me, would I have come out at all? My own mother seldom went into the garden. If I wanted a picnic like other children, she told Maude to pack biscuits and Coca-Colas into a basket and take me down to the lower lawn. Sometimes, she would wave to us from the verandah, as if we had gone to Jameson Park or down to the beach like everyone else.

But between my mother and Maude, there was only me, never a man. If they fought, I was the one who tried to have Maude singing again. I would knock on her door, carrying a brush-and-comb set my mother had given me, or my bottle of Wild Gardenia.

"Go away," she would say, "it's my off now."

"But I've got a present for you."

"Go away."

"I've never been able to stick a sulker," my mother would say, as Maude came in with the drinks tray. "Don't you ever be a sulker, do you hear? she would say, stroking my head in her lap. "Sulkers belong at the bottom of the lake, like worms in the mud."

And then, when I came into the kitchen after supper, Maude would go to the sink or the stove, turning her back to me. "You tell her *she's* the worm who sulks," she would say. "You tell her to learn her *own* lessons."

When the sun begins to set in the afternoon, I go out onto my terrace to look at the sea. At home, there was hardly half an hour of dusk before the sudden darkness came on. But now, I come out to watch the long fading of the light, and to see whether any ships are passing. I look at them the way we used to look out of the library window at school, watching the Rangston girls going home for the day. Their drivers would be waiting with biscuits and bottles of juice for them. And we each chose the girl we hated the most. Mine had red hair and freckles, and she was plump, like me.

I open my arms wide to the sun like a savage. Every afternoon, I take off my clothes and come out into it naked. It is as if the sun itself has become my lover, warming me like a lamp. If someone on a ship could see me, I would still stand as I am standing now, with my arms and legs wide. I am nineteen and a half, and I feel that any minute I will be old, that it is almost too late already.

I lean over the railing and stare down at the sea. It is lovely down there, green and smooth and shining. Sometimes, I can smell it all the way up here, and sometimes, if the wind is right, I can smell the orangefruit rotting at the back of the villa. But today an animal is crying somewhere, low and harsh, and I turn my head to listen. I walk along the terrace, straining to hear it over the wind in the scrub. It seems to be coming from the villa itself, so I look up. Naim's windows are open. It is coming from his tower.

At first I don't see her in the dim light, but then there she is on his footstool, sobbing, bent over herself like a huge black crow. I wait in the doorway until she sits up at last, resting her elbows on her knees and staring at something that she is holding in her hands. It is Naim's maroon silk cravat, the one he wears with his navy smoking jacket. She buries her face in it again, sobbing pitifully.

I have sobbed for my mother like this. I have sunk into the misery of it as if it were a pool, and stayed down there on purpose, trying never to breathe again. Perhaps we could stay like this ourselves until Naim returned — she crying, me watching. Nothing in this place seems impossible to me anymore. I have seen a cow drinking from the udder of another cow. And the rabbits do sit in the trees. I know this because, if I come too close, they jump down and hop away.

Sonja sits up, looking around for her glasses. They have fallen on the floor beside her. I would tell her where they were, but I want to go on watching. The monkey is watching, too, silent for once on top of the wardrobe. Sonja tucks the cravat into the pocket of her skirt and gets down onto her hands and knees, crawling like a baby.

I step up to her then, and she jumps back, blinking. Without glasses, her eyes are black as silk. Even in the gloom, I can see that her lashes are thick and long, and her eyes themselves are beautiful, with eyebrows that arch perfectly along the verge of her forehead.

I snatch up the glasses and point to her pocket, hold out my hand for the cravat. But she ducks away from me, as if I will hit her. Her nose and her lips are swollen from crying, and she has scratched her hands raw. They are enormous, like Naim's, and so are her feet. I step closer, still holding out my hand. At any moment, she could lunge and scratch me the way she has scratched herself, but I don't step back. I cock my head to listen to the evening wind. Naim loves to hear it moaning around his tower. It is the music of the gods, he says. It has come to serenade us.

She pulls the cravat from her pocket and flings it at me. I lift it with my foot, pick it up between two fingers like something foul. Then I throw her glasses at her as if she were a dog. I watch her grope for them and put them on, folding them behind her ears. They are thick and black and they flash up at me like teeth. But she can see me now, standing there naked, waving his cravat at her. I want her to remember me like this every time she thinks of Naim. I want it always to be part of her punishment.

6

Maude sees him turn as they drive through the gate on Sunday morning, but she stares ahead of her, stiff and straight. He will blame her, she knows. Everyone in the kitchen will blame her, but what do they know about Nalia?

If Nalia found out about Sonny, she would go straight to the manager and shout, and Sonny would be given the sack. He is a cheeky baboon, but he was wearing a hat for her today, and a nice white shirt, and she can't help it, she would rather be walking along the dusty road with him.

She stares down at her hands. They are freckled and lumpy and she doesn't know why he's after her. Still, men have been after her before. All those years in the big house, they would come to the back gate and ring the bell, but she never let them in. She never talked to them in the street either. She believed what Nalia told her about men. And anyway, what did she want with a husband, drinking and dirty and spending all her money?

But now, in this mountain place, Maude has had enough of her life. Dorothy is always saying that they will grow old together, they will go and live in a Home with their savings. But Maude doesn't want to spend her savings living in a Home. And she doesn't want Dorothy for her old age either, with her sharp nose looking into everyone else's business. What she wants is everything back the way it was, so that she doesn't feel so sorry for that baboon at the gate.

What has happened to her up here? Her heart is sore for everything, even for this madwoman, this crazy woman who follows any rubbish into the bush whenever she feels like it, and won't let her sing in the cottage, won't let anyone do what they want to do.

"We're early for a change," Nalia says.

A white priest is standing at the door of the little church. Nalia nods to him, but doesn't stop to talk. She is always rude like this, coming in here like a queen, without even a scarf or a hat. But who will tell her how to behave? That priest is going to take her hand on the way out and ask her to come again next time. The people will smile at her, too, as if she might give them money or a job.

"You sit over there," says Nalia, pointing to the other side of the church. She looks up at the ceiling to check the acoustics, then settles herself halfway down, on the aisle. From here she will be able to hear, and also to see their bodies swaying, loose, and the voices full and brilliant. The church is already dense with dark, gleaming bodies seasoned with cold cream and Lifebuoy soap. And over everything there is the lovely smell of dust and whitewash and candles burning.

Nalia closes her eyes to the thought of Sunday mornings at the river, the drive up the coast afterwards for lunch. Until the slimming salon took hold of the girl, Sundays were perfect. They would sit on the hotel verandah, the girl chattering so much that she had to be reminded to eat her crayfish sandwich. But as soon as she found an audience for her body, she couldn't wait for lunch to be over so that she could change into her red bikini and walk down the steps to the pool. Those steps were perfect for the purpose, curving behind a patch of wild bananas and then into full view, with two more flights to go. At the bottom she would choose a chaise, and then place it so that it faced the hotel, and also the old men in shorts and long socks, putting down their beers to watch her.

Was it the old men, then, who were always the danger? Nalia looks across the aisle at a woman with a small boy at her side. He is combed and greased, and he is singing, too. She has never longed for other people's lives, but now she wants to be this woman. She wants to silence the voice that seems to murmur along her blood day and night, waking her out of sleep at eleven minutes past three every morning.

If the girl were to come home, would the voice go away? Probably not. Katzenbogen would say that it has been there all along, only now she is paying attention to it. But what does he know? He can't hear how it seems to pose her whole life as a question. When the girl was home, there seemed to be no need for such a question. But now that she is gone, Nalia is back with herself, like a visitor — someone who has come out of the shadows and is trying to remember her own name.

Sonny is waiting when Maude comes out of the church. She sees his hat on the other side of the crowd, so she turns away, she steps to the side to wait for Nalia.

But he comes over to find her. "You saw me at the gate, hey?" he says. He is not joking anymore, he is gruff and cross.

Maude glances back for Nalia, but she is still talking to the priest. "She can make bad trouble," she whispers, "she can report you."

"That old chimpanzee? What can she do to me?"

"She's not a bad woman. She's had troubles."

"What's wrong with you, man? She goes with the mule man whenever she wants to."

"Maude?"

"Shh!" Maude hisses. "I can come down to the courts after tea."

"Maude? There you are!" Nalia is cutting across the grass towards them. "Ah! Wasn't it sublime?" She takes Maude's arm, she lays her head on her shoulder. "Oh Maude," she cries, "what would I do without you, my dear old friend?"

Maude knows this mood. The singing always puts Nalia in high spirits. But even so, it makes Maude happy to have Nalia's soft skin against hers again, and the smell of her hairspray, and people looking on in amazement.

"I'm a stupid old cow and a vain old scarecrow," Nalia says. "But we've put up with each other all these years, hey? We can be stupid old cows together."

The mood lasts for the rest of the day. Nalia orders a bottle of wine with her lunch, and offers Maude a glass, urges her to try it for once.

Maude shakes her head. Anything could happen with Nalia in this mood. Once, Nalia decided, half an hour before she was to leave for inland, that she would take Maude with her. They would stop on the way at Maude's village to visit her mother, Nalia would drop her off there, pick her up on the way back. It didn't matter to her that Maude didn't want to go, that Maude's mother was a drinker, always asking for money, sending Maude's brothers to town to ring at the gate bell and make a fuss. Nalia gave her ten minutes to pack her suitcase, and off they went together.

Nalia links her hands behind her head and creaks back in her chair. "As soon as I have word that she's coming home, we'll go back," she says. "I promise."

Maude nods. She has been counting the months herself. Maybe the girl isn't writing anymore because she has her own babies now. Or maybe the husband won't let her. Who can know what is going on with these mad people? Every night, she prays for the girl, and for the babies, and to bring them all home quickly.

"What's the time?" Nalia asks. "No! Let me guess! Half past two?"

Maude blushes. How can she go down to the courts when Nalia knowing everything, like a witch?

"Tonight," Nalia announces, "I shall tell them that I am considering a concert. That ought to please them after all these months, don't you think? What should I wear? The black lace again? Or the beige silk?"

Eventually, the wine puts Nalia to sleep in the verandah chair, so fast asleep that Maude cannot wake her to lead her to the bed. So she takes off her sandals and walks down the steps in her stockinged feet. She sits on the pillar at the bottom to put the sandals back on again, and then walks across the lawn like a cat.

When she gets to the courts, he is waiting. He has a mug of

tea for her, and two tennis biscuits on a tin plate. She takes the mug, although she would like him to know that she always has tea in a cup and saucer at home, and that Nalia is not just an old chimpanzee who goes off with the mule man whenever she wants to. She is famous, he can see her picture in the papers anytime he wants to.

The tea is lukewarm and too sweet. She drinks it quickly. Then she takes out her knitting and starts to count the stitches.

"Every month," he says, "I'm paying off on a car."

She looks up. He is sitting uneasily on the edge of one of the wicker chairs, all his cheekiness gone.

"For a taxi," he says.

"Where can you go here in a taxi?"

"Not here, man — in town. I got a house in Wentworth. My sister's living in it now."

"You got children?"

"A boy and girl. But they are grown up, they leave me alone."

Maude considers this information as she begins to knit. He has a sister and two children. He has a house in Wentworth. And he's saving up for a taxi.

"Don't knit, honey," he says. "Let's talk, hey?"

For the second time that afternoon, her cheeks flare up. Only men in the street have called her "honey" before. But this one isn't rude like they are. He is greedy for talk, greedy for her to talk to him. She stops her knitting, but, even so, she can't make herself look up.

"Thursday afternoons I'm off," he says. "What about you?"

"Only Sundays, but I can ask."

She can ask, but what will she tell Nalia? If Nalia knows there's a man here, it will be terrible, terrible. And yet, if she lies, Nalia is sure to find out. Every time she found the girl lying, there was horrible screaming and throwing, and it was always Maude who had to take the girl into her room and comfort her there, let her play with the rosary and the statue of the Virgin.

"We can go to the tearoom down the road, I can show you around."

Even the sound of his voice makes her feel like a traitor. When the girl's father would come to the house for dinner, his voice would curl down the passage, past the pantries, right into the kitchen and down her ears like the Devil himself. After dinner, he would come there to give her a tip, but she would always hand it on to the boy as soon as he left. Until the girl was snatched away and Nalia went mad, she always believed what Nalia told her about men.

"I'm Roman Catholic," she says.

He stares down at his cigarette. His forehead is shiny, he is going a bit bald. "Don't try to put me off," he says.

Maude has always wondered what would happen if she had to choose between staying with Nalia and taking a chance. If she stays, how does she know what Nalia will do for her? One minute she promises this and that, and the next she is threatening to sack her with nothing. If you stay with a madwoman, Dorothy says, you get what's coming to you. Dorothy never wants to listen when Maude talks about the good times with Nalia. She is jealous maybe. If she knew about this headwaiter, she'd go straight to the priest.

"There's lots of rubbish girls here," he says, looking at her again. "I saw you that first day, the way you walk so proud. A chap can get lonely for a proud woman, you know."

❧ 7 ❧

For three days, I have been listening for Sonja's bathwater. Twice a week, after supper, she runs herself a bath. It is the time of day I like best, with the bats out, and the air still warm. Usually, I sit on the terrace, writing in my notebook in the last of the light. But now I am waiting inside for the pipes to begin their clang and shudder.

Since I caught her crying in Naim's room, she avoids me. If I come down the passage, she turns and goes in the other direction. So I hunt her like an animal just to see how close I can get before she turns. I want her to know that, as long as she is here, I will hunt her like this. I will hunt her for my children, for anything I want.

Today, I want the key to Naim's study. I have seen her taking her monkey in there. And she puts on his music, too, while I have to stand outside listening, knowing that I am his wife and she is only his half-sister.

As soon as I hear the pipes, I fly out of my room and along the passage to the nursery door. The children are sleeping already, the nurses have gone to their room. And so I slip in and stop only for a moment to look at them. I have never been into this room; it is part of Sonja's suite, and is built out over the cliff like Naim's, with leaded windows all around, and a glass skylight that can be opened in hot weather. When I first came to this island, I came in here. But I didn't want the rooms for myself. They were too cold with all that glass. Everything on the island was cold then.

The children sleep in one large cot, clasped together like Siamese twins. I lean over the side and breathe them in, sour milk and porridge. I long to lift them out and run. But where would I go? How would I even get through the gates of the villa?

I turn away and walk through to Sonja's room. It is a chaos of suitcases, and at first, I think she must be leaving at last. But then I see that nothing ever seems to have been unpacked. The suitcases are pushed against the tallboy and there is a pile of washing between them. Her day dress is thrown over a chair, and her big black shoes, still laced, are kicked off here and there.

She is splashing in the bath, grunting like an animal, and the monkey is gibbering in there, too. I lift her dress and pull the keys quickly from the left pocket. They are on a ring, just like Maude's, and the ring is attached to a brown leather strap. I have seen that strap around her wrist every day, but until now, I have never seen the keys themselves.

I carry them over to the chair and stare down at them. Every key has a small brass disc attached to it, with letters engraved that I cannot read. Some of the keys are big, like ours, old-fashioned and straight, but there are smaller ones too, more modern ones, all bunched together in the middle.

I know the key to his study. It is long and flat, like the key to our kist at home, but thicker, heavier. All my life, I have noticed keys. I like to know where they fit, how they work. "What do you need your own keys for?" my mother would shout. "When you're old enough for keys, you'll be old enough to understand a lot of things."

There is a splash and a thud from the bathroom, the water beginning to run out. I move quickly through the bunch until I find the study key. Then I slip it off the ring, and slide the rest back into her pocket.

His study is always a surprise after the cold stone of the villa — warm, even without a fire. I go to the curtains to breathe them in. They smell of sun and dust, just like ours, and I am about to draw them when I hear the sisters. I run to the side window to look. They are making off across the kitchen lawn together, with their scarves tied under their chins, and the double basket in which they bring food from the village every day.

So this is why Naim never wants me in here until they have gone home for the night. If I say I would like to come to listen to music after supper, he draws the curtains, even though it isn't dark yet. There is nothing to see out there, he says, and I have believed him. I have believed that the sisters arrive out of nowhere, like ghosts, and go back like ghosts as well.

But now here they are, talking loudly, and I open the window and climb out onto the grass below. The air is warm and sweet outside, and the rabbits are out as usual, the night birds are singing. I run along the side of the house, under the eaves, never letting the sisters out of my sight. Just as they reach the fence, the older one takes a key out of her pocket, I can see it glinting in the thin evening light. I come closer, but their backs are to me and the fence itself is in shadow. And then, suddenly, they are through it, they are on the other side, squawking to each other like a pair of Indian mynahs.

I wait for them to disappear, and then run up to the fence and stare at it, walk along it, shaking each post, each rail. But there is no sign of a gate, nor did I hear one open or shut. When Maude unlocked our padlock, anyone could hear the crack of the metal, the chain clang down. When she pushed the gate itself, it screeched like an animal and the whole fence shook. I would look back at the house before I went through it. I would stare at it in the full morning light as if I could burn it onto my eyes. But this fence is silent and solid and unmovable. The sisters have passed through it like ghosts after all.

All night, I lie curled up in Naim's smoking jacket on the divan. Without him, it is only a divan, sloping and uncomfortable, and I hardly sleep, I just float lightly, passing along the passages of the villa, in and out of the rooms. And then, suddenly, as if I have been searching for it all along, I wake with a start to the thought of the liquor cabinet — the keys that I have seen hanging on the inside of the door. I switch on the lamp and run over to it, pull the doors open. And there they are — row after row of them hanging from hooks.

As soon as it is light, I go back to the fence and walk along it, running my hands down each post, along each rail. When I find the gate, it is like nothing — like a shadow of itself, a thin line in the metal like a hair under my finger. I slide my hand under the rail to find the lock, and, when I do, crouch down to see what kind of key it will take. I can hear the nurses in the kitchen now, they are making breakfast for the children. But they cannot see me. There is no window that looks out on this part of the fence; it is hidden from everything but the stone walls of the villa.

I lay all the keys out on the ground. There are only five that would fit such a lock, and I work through them until one slips in and I can turn it. When I do, the gate glides open silently, impossibly silent, a small segment of fence on invisible hinges. Even when I walk through it and pull it closed behind me, I can hardly hear it click.

And then, from outside, I stop to look back at the villa. It could be any normal place, just a villa on a hill, with the sun rising onto it, royal palms, and a fountain, and a beautiful tropical garden. If I were a normal person, I would wonder who lived there, and what their lives were like in such a place. But I am not normal. I have the key to the gate in one pocket, and in the other I have cashews from Naim's bowl. I take a few out and eat them as I walk. They are the taste of Naim himself, and of the island, and of this walk down the mountain, free and easy.

❧ 8 ❧

Nalia has delayed announcing a concert. There is a new woman in the place, who has brought her own coffee beans with her and has the kitchen grind them up and deliver the coffee to her table, very thick and black. She is small and straight, and she instructs the headwaiter to turn the gramophone down or to switch it off entirely.

Maude has found out from the staff that she has come from overseas. Certainly, her clothes aren't local. She dresses like an organ grinder's monkey, and she has a little dog that she keeps in her handbag. She takes food from her plate and feeds it to the creature, which Nalia considers a revolting display. Nalia stands up after pudding and tells the headwaiter to have her coffee brought out onto the verandah.

While she waits out there, she stares into the darkness. Ghost man or no ghost man, she could do with a talk to Katzenbogen. What she would like is to hear her own voice reading him the words she has written. When she reads them aloud, they seem to tell a new story, settle her into another view of her life. And then, later, when he tells the story back to her, it is different all over again. That is what she misses up here.

Tomorrow, she decides, she will telephone him and tell him to come up for the weekend. Who cares if it is unorthodox? He is always looking behind him like a frightened rabbit on the two-block walk to the hotel. Unorthodox, irregular, unprofessional — what are these words to her? Where were they when he bound up her feet with rags? When he told her that he would follow her wherever she chose to go?

But when she gets back to the cottage, she finds that the telephone lines are down again, nothing can get through. She slams the receiver onto the cradle and barks at Maude. "One of these days," she says, "we'll just pack up and go home."

Maude nods. She knew it would happen like this. The minute she wants to stay, Nalia wants to go. And there won't even be time to explain to Sonny.

Nalia flings off her clothes and goes to stand naked in front of the mirror. After all the months of calisthenics, her body is supple. She can fold herself down, touching her forehead to her knees. She can reach all the way back too, arching into a perfect curve, her hands on the ground behind her. When the ghost man sees this, he gives out a low whistle. But what is her body to him? The shape and shadow of a woman? An old woman bending herself back for him? Sometimes, with his smell and his grunting, she can't help it, she is the girl herself being plundered like this. And she can hardly breathe with the sadness of it all, of all the girls she saw split open with knives, the ones used like dogs and fed like dogs until they got sick and died.

One mother managed to keep her daughter to herself. She kept her bread for her. She stole for her and fought for her, and even so, when the soldiers were coming in to free them at last — even when the girl was all bones and lice, freezing and starving — even then, one of the soldiers was coming for her, unbuttoning his trousers, what did he care? But the mother pushed the girl down and sat on her like a bald old hen. She sat on her daughter and stared up at the soldier out of her dark sockets, stared and stared until the other soldiers saw her and came and pulled him away.

Nalia had hated that girl then. She had hated the mother, too. Once, when she was eight or nine, her own grandmother found her at the back of the garage, opening her legs so that the chauffeur could look inside her. He didn't touch, he only wanted to sit on his chair and unbutton himself and look at her. Nalia liked him to do this. He had a little room back there, quite dark even though there was a window onto the kitchen garden. He would ask her politely to take off her pants and climb onto the table for him. And then, when they drove out in the car, he never looked back at her through the mirror. He never looked at her at all unless she was on his table.

But when her grandmother found her there, she screamed. She screamed so loudly that all the servants came running. And then, when Nalia's mother woke from her afternoon rest and called for the car, he was gone. He had run away without even taking his clothes. When Nalia saw him again, he was wearing a soldier's uniform and leaning out of the truck window to offer the guard a cigarette. He could have looked up and seen her watching him, but he didn't. He had grown a moustache, and his hair was beginning to go grey, and he was smiling.

"Ma'am?" Maude holds out her nightdress, warmed in front of the electric heater.

But Nalia goes to sit naked at the piano. She picks out the old song that the girl used to love, and Maude sits down to listen. She loves the song, too, although the girl could never stand her to sing it herself. She was spoilt that way, rude like the mother. Even the African children are allowed to sing Nalia's songs. When she goes off with the mule man, they dance behind her, singing together. And then, when she comes back, they are waiting on the rock again like monkeys, gibbering and laughing.

Nalia closes the piano and goes out onto the verandah to stretch. The night is beautifully cold. This morning there was snow on the mountains, and tomorrow there could be more. Already, she has forgotten the new woman. She has forgotten Katzenbogen too. And the ghost man. And the girl herself. It is lovely to be able to forget like this, to be unable to think of the name or the reason for anything, if only for the moment — for the time that she is singing.

The next day, everything goes wrong. First, Nalia decides that she and Maude will walk to the supply store for sweets after lunch. So they set off, with the children capering behind them, shouting out rude things. When Maude turns to scold them, they pull faces at her and Nalia laughs.

By the time they get back and Nalia lies down for her rest, it is too late for Sonny. But Maude goes down there anyway. She tries to knit, but she can't help looking up for him every minute. And then the new woman's dog comes running around her feet, jumping and laddering her stockings.

"Get off!" Maude shouts. "Get away, you ugly thing!"

The new woman is calling it, calling and calling, but the dog runs in the other direction, like a rat.

It is hopeless. Sonny won't come, now that the new woman

is down here. Maude is about to pack up her knitting when she hears the woman scream, high and loud and terrible. She stands up to see what the matter is. By the time she reaches the top of the steps, Nalia is out on the verandah, too, still in her dressing gown.

"What's going on?" she calls out.

There is a crowd now on the other side of the garden wall — a few of the children, and Sonny, and two of the gardeners — all staring up at the sky, pointing and shouting. The new woman is there, too, screaming still, with the dog's leash in her hands.

"Hello?" Nalia walks through the gate and over to the crowd. She is watching the new woman scream the way she watches a spider cross a tablecloth. Nalia will never let Maude kill a spider, not even the big ones. "Waiter!" she calls out. "Come here!"

Maude sees Sonny run to her, she sees him shake his head sadly, and point at the new woman, talking, talking.

But then Nalia cuts him off. "Two double brandies, please. Come on," she says, taking the woman's arm. "Come inside with me."

"The eagle got the dog just now," Sonny whispers to Maude as he passes. "Down there by the rock."

Maude stops to see if it's a joke. She looks up into the sky too. She has seen eagles floating around up there like devils. "*Hau,* shame for the dog," she says.

"Shame what!" Sonny snaps.

"Sonny!" The manager has arrived. "What are you doing down here?"

"Getting an order for the stewie, *baas.*"

"Well get on with it then."

Maude stares at the manager. Nalia is famous for her shouting. But when she shouts, she shouts the same at everyone, high and low. And here is this man now, shouting at Sonny like he was a rubbish, and Sonny just smiling, running like a dog himself.

When Maude comes into the cottage, the new woman is lying on the couch. Now that she has been crying, Maude can see that she is older than she thought. She is like an old woman who has lost her child.

"Take off your shoes," Nalia says. She is always bossy when something bad happens. One time, when Maude broke her leg running down the hill for the bus, Nalia bossed her way right to the front of the line at the hospital. She bossed Maude into bed afterwards, too, and she got the electrician to put in a bell like hers, down to the kitchen. Maude had to ring for the housegirl if she wanted the potty or anything. She had to lie there like a dead person, whether she liked it or not, until the leg got better.

The old woman begins to unlace her boot.

"Good." Nalia drops the boot to the floor. "Now the other one."

"You are kind," the new woman says. Her voice is high, like a little girl's, and her stockings have holes in them.

"I am not kind at all, I have never been kind."

Sonny knocks and comes in with the brandy. Then he lingers in the shadow of the wall. He knows just how to stand back so that nobody will notice him.

"What happened this afternoon?" he whispers to Maude.

"We went to the supply store," she whispers back. "Maybe she's had enough of this place. Maybe we'll be leaving soon."

"I've had enough too. Give me your number in town."

"Why did I come back here?" the woman wails, gulping her brandy. She still has the leash in her hands and is looking at it pitifully. "I never really wanted to come back here at all," she says.

Nalia grunts. Regret is a luxury she has never allowed herself. People who say, "If I had my life to live again" should be made to live it, knowing just what lies ahead. "What did you do overseas?" she asks.

"Failed, failed."

The brandy is doing its work. When the woman came screaming into view, like Medea, it was as if she had been delivered to Nalia, stripped of her coffee beans and her mad overseas clothes. Tonight, Nalia will order dinner for both of them down here. The telephone lines will be down until Tuesday, the manager says, but she doesn't mind that now. She might even let the woman hear her practising. There are any number of things that Nalia can do to show this woman who she is and how she herself has been lost to the world in this Godforsaken place.

9

The way down is not as steep as it looks from the funicular. The path zigzags along the rock face, following the edge of the gorge. The sun is only now rising full, and I stop at a stream to drink. Then I shake the dust out of my sandals and go on, singing as I walk.

It takes me over an hour to reach the bottom of the cliff face, where the path leads onto an unpaved road above the town. If Maude were here, we would be singing her hymns together. I can sing anything I like with Maude, and she will find the descant. I smile. I walk along a road, singing like any normal person, and I am as free as I have ever been in my dreams.

When I reach the edge of the town, I quieten down. A few mongrels come out of the shade to bark at me. They sniff my feet, my skirt, smelling the dogs from the villa. And then they dance behind me, barking at a safe distance. Except for them, everything is silent. The doors and the shutters of the houses are closed. Perhaps the people are still sleeping. Or perhaps it is their day of rest.

When I asked Naim what religion he was, he said that he is many things, he speaks many languages as well. My mother too speaks many languages, and she loves a new word, a new idea. Maybe that was what she loved about having the Syrian for dinner — the word itself, the idea behind the word. If she falls in love with a word, she will roll it around in her full, rich voice, and then pounce on it like a cat. If I write a word in my diary that is new to her, I have to explain everything about it to her, even if it is slang. But it is not only the meaning that she is after, it is the sound of the meaning. If they match to her liking, she will make the word her own. Sometimes, she will sit at the piano and sing it up and down the scale. And then she will look up, and we will laugh together.

I turn into an alley and lean against the wall. Even when she is silent, her voice is everywhere around me. Everything I see, I see for her. If she weren't behind my eyes, what would the blues and reds of the shutters look like, gleaming in the morning light? What would I have seen when I saw the Syrian down there on the terrace?

I follow the alley down the hill, turning here and there, keeping the sun in front of me. The town is a labyrinth of alleys running downhill, the steeper ones turning into steps. Every now and then, I catch a glimpse of the water, blinding in the morning sun. As I approach the bottom, I hear women's voices, children too. And then, suddenly, turning into a larger alley, I am in a crowd of people — women walking in groups and carrying double baskets, children running behind them.

The women themselves have broad faces, black hair, and small wide eyes, like the sisters. They are wearing homemade floral dresses, or homemade skirts and nylon blouses in bright colours. I know that they have seen me, but they don't smile, they don't even look at me. Only the children come up to have a look at me. One darts a hand out to touch me, but a woman grabs him back and gives him a slap.

Still, I walk among them, invisible. It must be the way tourists walk when they go to new places. The Brazilian girl on the ship told me that she had gone with her family to see a native village, and bought beadwork there, and carvings. If I had money, I would buy things here, whatever they were. I have always longed for money to spend like that, and to catch a bus on my own, without Maude — to pay for the ticket myself, and get off at Joubert Street, and go into the Bon Marché. I would go straight to the haberdashery department and choose what I wanted, even if it were only a pin cushion to take to my mother as a present.

We pass small shops that open onto the alley, and I stop here or there to have a look. The shopkeepers do not call to me as they call to the women. I can move down the alley with the crowd, or I can stop and look at bolts of fabric or plastic sandals if I want to. I stop, but I don't touch. I don't want anything to make them notice me. I want to move like a ghost with the crowd, down to the end of the alley, to the small plaza there, where there are stalls selling food — baskets of fish, and the strange fruit of the island, dried meat hanging from a hook, and, from another, a small dried monkey. The women move from stall to stall, shouting, waving off the flies. Flies hover in a cloud over everything here, and the place smells sweet and rank.

At first, I don't see what the men are doing in the middle of the plaza. But then I see the blood running over the cobblestones, the calf they have killed and laid out on a stone platform in the middle. Another is waiting with a rope around its neck.

Women stand to the side, shouting things out. The men nod, their knives flashing. They grunt as they work, throwing the bloodied meat into a large tin trough.

I try to back away, but the crowd is packed firmly behind me now. The whole place has been built like a stage, with the killing platform high in the middle and the cobblestones sloping away from it. The women stand just beyond the gutter that circles the plaza, but still their feet are splashed with blood. I am splashed myself. I turn to push my way back up the alley, and there, right across the entrance, are the sisters with their basket.

They stare past me like all the others. And then one calls something out to the men, and everyone falls silent. She makes her way up to the platform and points, waits there until she is given what she wants. And then she goes back to her sister and the women clear a path for them, so that they can go back up the alley together.

I follow quickly after them, before the women can close me in again. As soon as my back is turned, they laugh, loud and raucous. But I hurry behind the sisters until I am free of the crowd. And then, as soon as I can, I turn down an alley towards the harbour. I can see the sun there, glinting silver off the water, and I want to wash my feet in it, I want to feel the water on my skin. But there is an old man on a donkey coming towards me and I have to flatten myself against the wall to let him pass. He is ragged and ugly, like all of them, and when he is alongside me, he stops the donkey. He stares down at me through his milky eyes, toothless, chewing on something. Then, suddenly, he hawks and spits, and his saliva lands full on my neck.

I grab Naim's jacket and wipe furiously. But my skin and my blouse are damp and loathsome, my sandals are still sticky with blood. I push past the donkey and run down the alley, gasping, shuddering. When I reach the harbour, I stop and lean against a wall until I can breathe properly again.

The children are there already, swimming in the water. There are fishing boats tied up in a row, and, farther down, the motorboat on its own dock. It is bigger than I remember, rising out of the water like the beak of an enormous bird. I begin to walk towards it, but when the children see me, they climb out of the water and caper around me in a naked pack. I try to smile at them, but they only grin back at me in an ugly parody.

And then, suddenly, a shutter bangs open behind us, and we all turn. It is the house I had noticed on my first day — taller, different from the rest. A woman has come onto the upstairs balcony and is staring out into the harbour. She looks nothing like the island people. Her skin is as pale as my mother's, and her hair is not tied into a scarf. The house itself is elegant, with gables and fretwork and a carved front door.

One of the older boys swaggers under the balcony with his hands on his hips, and they all laugh. They settle themselves into rowdy groups along the docks to watch us both. I look up at her, but she won't smile, she won't look at me, either. She just holds on to the rail and stares past me, out at the water. When I turn to see what she is looking at, the children laugh again. And so I cross the road to her front door and lift the knocker.

10

The new woman is a singing coach out to pasture. She wouldn't have come back at all if her third husband hadn't gambled away all her money. Now all she has left are these ridiculous clothes that he talked her into, and a small stipend from the opera house. If she had stayed on there, she says, he would have wheedled that out of her as well.

Nalia huffs in her chair. When the woman isn't talking about husbands or dogs, she is hard and sharp and unrelenting. Which roles? she asks Nalia. Which directors? But when Nalia mentions her years at the Conservatoire, everything that she had to give up when the War came, the woman waves them away as if such a past does not deserve remembering. "Why haven't I seen you in the dining room?" she asks. "Or at those so-called concerts?"

Nalia shrugs off the question. She talks instead of the university lecturer who is writing up the story of her life, of the house up on the hill that she has left draped and locked. She talks of the view of the bay, and the garden rolling down the hill.

The woman closes her eyes. "Oh!" she cries, "oh to be protected like that!"

"*Protected?*" Nalia barks. "Protected by whom?"

The woman drops her jaw slightly. She has thick lips and her skin is dry as dust. "Darling," she says to Nalia, "just look at me."

Nalia looks, and yes, it is a revolting sight. Suddenly she wants her own life back the way it was. Except for the girl, everything is still in place — the dogs in the kennel, Braughton seeing that the garden is properly done. She will leave on Wednesday, she decides. And she will take the woman with her. To have such a woman there — proud, ruined, grateful — to have such a hand in her life again — this would be worth all the trouble in the world.

She looks at her watch and the woman sits up on cue, reaches for her boots, and pulls them back on.

"Maude!" Nalia calls out, "Bring the torch and take this lady back up to the hotel, please."

Maude has been waiting on the other side of the door for this. All these years, Nalia has never had time for anyone else's troubles. So why pick up this old woman now, like the eagle picked up the dog? If the woman isn't careful, she'll be eaten up the same way. All the way up the hill, she asks Maude questions about Nalia. But Maude knows better than to answer. Right from the start, Nalia taught her what to say when someone asks questions. Either you say you don't know, or you suggest that maybe she should ask Nalia herself.

"Give me your number in town," Sonny says. "I gave my notice already."

Maude hands him a slip of paper. She has been carrying it around in her apron pocket all morning. "But you can't phone me there," she says.

"Then what must I do? I got no phone myself." He taps his foot impatiently.

All night, Maude has been considering this question. There are three phones in the house, but Nalia can hear them all. And even if Sonny could phone her, then what? What about Dorothy? What about the church? Before Sonny, she could sleep at night, and she could still hear everything, she was always proud of that. But now she lies awake in the dark, thinking only of the future, thinking of Sonny.

Suddenly, he has taken her hand in his. He has reached over and taken it, and there is no taking it back. They sit in silence like this until she says, "Usually, on Tuesdays, she goes inland. But we're going to have the other one there now, I don't know what's going to happen."

"If I phone and someone's there, just say, 'You got the wrong number,'" he says.

Maude is so relieved that he is not trying to argue her into more than this that she could close her eyes right now and sleep. "My off is Wednesday, after lunch," she says.

"And Sunday?"

"Sunday is church." She doesn't mention Dorothy, she doesn't want to think about Dorothy now. The hand he is holding feels stiff and hot. She wants to move her fingers, but he'll think she wants it back.

"I joined the Methodists," he says. "I got fed up with those priests and all their rubbish. They don't want you to be happy. Why not?"

She bows her head. Dorothy would tell her that he is the voice of the Devil. Dorothy sees the Devil everywhere.

"You've got one life, man, you got to be happy." He releases her hand at last, and gets the cigarette from behind his ear. "The Methodists sing so beautiful," he says. "I want to hear you singing those hymns with your beautiful voice."

Maude flushes. She has sung those hymns herself. On their way down to the beach, she and Dorothy like to stop outside St. Giles Road Methodist Church to listen. "Rock of Ages, cleft for me," and "Now thank we all our God," and "O Jesus, I have promised." And he is right, she has wanted to join in right there. As it is, she and Dorothy sing them together as they walk down the hill, with Maude always taking the high part. Since they were girls, they have sung like this. As long as they are singing, Dorothy never talks about the Devil.

The last morning, when Nalia goes out onto the lawn, they are all there waiting — the African children, the ghost man, too. At home, she will go down onto the lower lawn before breakfast. But it won't be the same without the mountains, without the man, or the children, or the ghost of her grandmother everywhere around her. The old woman is there even in the smell of the ghost man's tobacco. But mostly she is there when Nalia takes off down the path to the river. She is Nalia herself longing to follow them.

When they reach the opposite bank, the ghost man says, "You going away, I hear?"

"Shhh."

"I'm just asking. You going away?" He has stopped in the

shadow of the cliff and is trying to look into her face. "I'm *asking* you," he says again.

She turns to leave. "I'm going back to the cottage," she says.

But he grabs her wrist and swings her hard, pushes her against the cliff.

"What do you think you're *doing?*" she cries. But she knows already. She has felt it in the fury of his gait, the way she had to force herself to follow him this morning.

He shoves her down onto her knees with both hands, holds her there while he fumbles his shorts open. Then he grabs her hair and pulls her face towards him.

"Open!" he growls. He jabs himself against her lips, against her teeth. *"Open!"* he shouts.

Her head is spinning with the stink of him, and with this morning's breakfast, vomit in her throat. She tries to turn her head away, but he clasps her jaw expertly between thumb and finger so that she has to open her mouth, and, when she does, he pushes himself in, slamming her head back against the rock, lifting her chin and holding it in place.

She tries to open her throat wider. In her frenzy for air, she can't even feel the pain on her scalp, the blood soaking into her hair. All she wants is to tell him that she was wrong, she isn't ready for death after all. But he is saying something while he chokes her, he is chanting something at her, working himself to the end of this, to the final slam of her head against the cliff and the horrible pulsing down her throat.

"Money!" he is saying.

She is so faint that she hardly knows she can gasp. And then, when she does, she has to vomit — heaving and retching until there is nothing left but bile.

"Money!" he shouts. "I want money for this!"

She looks up at him. His eyes are red with drink or with dagga.

"Ugly old baboon, you think I want this from *you!?*" he shouts.

She can't speak yet, but she drops her eyes to his boots and opens her hands a little to show him that she has no money. She can hear him breathing. She knows this sort of silence. He wants to kill her. He wants the pleasure of it in his hands or his feet. They are always the instrument of death — the hands or the feet. But if she stays quite still like this, breathing invisibly, not moving her eyes from his boots, the moment might pass and he might go away, find something else to kill.

At last, he kicks her hard in the chest. Then he hawks, and spits full at her. She can feel the spittle warm on her forehead, down her cheek, and she would like to lift her hand and touch it, warm and wet, but she dare not.

"I'll come and find you in town," he says. "You better have some money for me then, or you watch out!"

Sonny is at the gate when they all drive out that afternoon. Maude can even turn to look because the old woman is in front, and she herself is sitting in the back, for once. All afternoon, he has been standing on the verandah, watching her pack the car.

Everyone knows by now that Nalia got a hiding from the mule man. The children saw her first, coming back up the path, and they ran to call Maude. But Nalia won't even report him, she won't talk about it, either. She is always like that. You think she'll do one thing and she won't. Maude was the one who had to make her sit down while she ran the bath, and then knelt there to wash her clean. Sitting there in the bath, silent, bowing her head so that Maude could wash off the blood, Nalia was an old, old woman. And then afterwards, while Maude dried underneath her breasts and put Mercurochrome on her head and her chest, she still said nothing. She just asked for some peroxide in water to gargle with, and for Maude to draw the curtains so that she could think.

Maude smiles. She can see that Sonny would run after the car if he could, that he would jump onto the bumper and go all the way to town with them, the cheeky baboon. She waves to the children next to the road, holding up their hands for sweets. She is happy that Nalia brought her to this place. And now she is even happy to be leaving.

❧ 11 ❧

The woman is blind. I know this only when I see her feel her way over the tray for the handle of the coffeepot. When she led me through the house and out into her walled garden, she did so without hesitating for a step or a threshold. When the village girl brought out the tray of coffee and stayed for a moment to stare at me, the woman knew this, too. She barked something at her and waved her off.

As soon as the girl is gone, she turns to me. "I was hoping you would come," she says.

I hear the words before I even know that I understand them. "Hoping?" I say.

"I have been waiting for you to come," she says. Her accent is rounder than Naim's, heavier too. Until now, he is the only one I have been able to speak to, the only one who understands me.

"I came because a man spat on me in the alley this morning," I say. But the truth is, had I known that she existed, I would have come straight here.

"The people here don't like strangers," she says.

"Why?"

"Naim, of course."

I hear his name in her mouth, the slide of her voice around it, and I am glad that she can't see the rush of blood to my face, the way I have to swallow before I can say, "I'm sorry, I don't know who you are."

We are sitting at a table in a corner of her garden. It is a small, walled garden, flowering everywhere. A fragrant creeper with enormous yellow flowers obscures the walls. It has wound itself into the tree that shades the table, and has filled the air so strongly that I can taste it in my coffee.

"If you don't know who I am, why did you come?"

"I saw you on your balcony," I say. I lift my arm to see if she will follow it, but she doesn't. So I stare at her openly. With her black hair and her pale skin, she looks like the Queen of Hearts. Even her face is in the shape of a heart — a sharp chin, and a high, broad forehead rising into two rounded peaks.

"Until he brought you here," she says, "I was the only one on the island."

The coffee rises, bitter and sour, to my throat. "The only what?" I say.

She sits back then, as if she is staring at me. Her eyes are not like a blind person's at all. They are a beautiful sea green, with a circle of black around them, and her hands lie perfectly still in her lap. "But now I hear that the sister is back."

"Do you know Sonja?"

"She was here before either of us. Everyone says that is what killed his mother."

Her words loop themselves around my throat and I can hardly swallow. "What do you mean?" I manage in a whisper.

She sighs. "The family is everything to Naim. It is the sadness of his life, but he can't help it, don't you see? And she was very young."

I think of Naim turning from Sonja to me with that smile of his — patient, bored, corrupt — of Naim with tears in his eyes, showing me the photograph of his mother.

She stands up and holds out a hand to take me inside. "You are still a child yourself," she says. "The women up there told me that."

I stay in the blind woman's house for thirteen days. We are not friends, nor are we enemies. I am here because I want him to find me here, and so does she. I wear her clothes and eat her food. When she brushes my hair, I close my eyes and her hands become Naim's hands on her hair.

"I have henna," she says, "it will thicken the hair."

She has the girl mix up a bowl of it, and then she smooths it on, combs it through. She is hard and rough like my mother, but she is also deft like her, and sure, and silent.

"He must know from Sonja that I'm here," I say at last.

"Of course he knows. But he is clever. Naim is the cleverest man on earth."

"Then why doesn't he come?"

"He will never walk into a trap of women. He will never ask for something he doesn't mean to get, or answer a question if he doesn't want to."

I don't tell her that he has answered mine. I wrap this knowledge around me like a shield — how he chose me, how he won me in a bet.

Sitting out in the garden while the henna sets, she tells me that the people hate Naim because he refuses to take their daughters. Until he brought me here, she says, they would send their daughters up the mountain anyway, hoping that one day he would keep one of them for himself. But he never has. He has no taste for the local people. When the sisters were girls, they too were sent up, and he took them in as servants, trained them like dogs. And now they are his spies, his dog spies, and everyone on the island leaves them alone. The same is true of the nurses. Even so, if my children ever came down here, the island people would kill them like animals, and drop them far out to sea so that no one would ever find out. That's how these people are, she says. They hate us that much.

I start as if I have been struck. Until now, I have forgotten the children as I forget a dream. But suddenly they are here, like a blow, a slash across my heart. "Who would bring them down?" I ask, hardly breathing.

She shakes her head. "No one will. No one would dare to."

The blow becomes an ache now. It is quite different from the ache that I suffer for my mother. That ache is also for myself — it is for my mother without me, for myself without her. But this is for the children alone. Perhaps, if they weren't mine — if I had never seen them from the beginning, never danced with them, or smelled them, or heard them laugh — I would be free of this, as Sonja must be free. I have seen her smile at them the way Maude used to smile at me — a pause, before passing on to the next thing.

"He won't send them away as he has sent mine," she says. "Yours?"

"Mine are boys. They don't count."

"But one of my children isn't even his!" I blurt out.

She laughs then, as if I have made a joke. "Other men are

nothing to Naim. He takes possession of them the way he takes possession of us."

But I am wild now to find the differences between us. I am his wife, she is not. "Have you ever been up to the villa?" I ask.

She shakes her head. "After the mother, it was the sister. And now it is you. The family is everything to Naim."

In the evening, when we sit in the garden, drinking the strange, sweet wine that the maid brings out, she tells me that she was born blind as a punishment for her own mother. As long as she can remember, she says, there was a man who used to come for her mother. He would arrive at their house with no notice and stay for a night or a week or a month. Her mother never bothered to close the door if it was hot. She didn't care about what could be heard by a blind girl.

But even if she covered her ears, the daughter could hear them from anywhere in the house. So she would go out into the garden to wait until it was over. And then, one day, the man brought Naim with him. While her mother and the man were upstairs, Naim came into the garden to find her. He took her face in his hands and traced it the way she herself traced everything she wanted to know. She leans over and runs her fingers around my face to show me how he did it, across my eyelids, down my cheeks. Her touch is even lighter than Naim's, and I know the whole story from it.

"Why don't you let me pierce your ears?" she says suddenly, fingering my earlobes.

"Fine," I say, thinking only of the touch of his fingers on her ears, the pearl drop earrings that he gave me.

She rings the bell and instructs the girl. And then out comes a tray with a needle, a bowl, a wad of cotton wool, and a silver hand mirror. Even then, I don't think of what is about to happen. And I forget her blindness, I forget it completely. I pick up the mirror and watch as she dips and wipes, squeezing the earlobe tight between her fingers, poising the point of the needle at the spot. And then, suddenly, without warning, stabbing it through.

"Still!" she says, "Be still!" She holds the needle in place while she slips off her own earring with her other hand. And then, in one movement, the needle is out and her earring is through. It burns there like magic, long and filigree, with seed pearls dangling along the bottom.

"Now the other one," she says.

I know that he gave her these earrings. Everything she has was given to her by him. But her clothes are nothing like mine. They are draped and foreign-looking, and her perfume is as pungent as the creeper in the garden. When Naim comes to fetch me, I will tell him that I want some of that perfume for myself. I want him to think of me whenever he comes to her. I want him to think of me with every woman he goes to.

"How did he find you?" she asks, sitting back now as if to admire her handiwork. The light is almost gone. Her face is as pale as the moon.

"He is my father's cousin."

She puts her wineglass down. "Who is your father?"

So I tell her about my mother, and the day my father came to her dressing room. I tell her about his launch and his women, and about the trousseau my mother embroiders just to annoy him, the stinking pit that he detests so much. When my mother and I walk down Joubert Street, I say, she always points out his women to me because they are nothing to her. They are less than nothing. They are a joke.

When I look over at her, I see that she is crying. Tears roll down her cheeks, onto her dress.

"Why are you crying?" I ask.

"Because life is sad."

My mother would scoff at this. She would pounce on the words and pull them to shreds, even if they came from a blind woman, a woman taken by the friend of her mother's lover, and brought to an island, and kept there without her children. My mother is the only one who is allowed to know about life's sadness, and I am sick of her taking the whole subject for herself. What does she know about blindness anyway? What does she know about any misery except her own beloved War?

And yet, I can't help it, when I repeat the phrase to myself, my mouth twists up in derision. I want to say, "Sad? As opposed to what?" I want to laugh as my mother would laugh, and to tell her that I was never allowed to feel sorry for myself, that my mother hates self-pity almost as much as she hates my father.

The blind woman wipes her eyes with her dress. Then she looks up and says, "The man who came to my mother was your father. He is my father too."

❧ 12 ❧

The motorboat arrives at midnight. I hear the engine roar in and cut out, the voices of the people swarming onto the wharf, and I lie in the dark, waiting. When he does come for me, when he climbs the stairs and opens the door, he will find me lying here with my eyes closed. He might whisper my name, but I won't answer. And then he will see the earrings, heavy and wonderful in my flaming earlobes.

When the blind woman heard the boat start up after supper, she said, "He will come back tonight." And then, when we had waited for two hours in the garden, she said, "We should go to bed. There is no point in waiting for Naim."

I creep over to the shutters and push one open a little. The harbour is floodlit as if it were morning. I can see the nose of the boat out there, and boxes piled on the dock in front of it. Men come one by one to carry them away, and there are women too, watching, calling things out. But I don't see Naim. I watch until the boxes are all gone and the crowd has gone with them. Then I push the shutter open and walk out onto the balcony.

The blind woman is there already, standing at the rail. They must have seen her, he must have seen her there himself. But the harbour is empty now, and I can hear the funicular clanging into place. The crowd has moved up there, talking, laughing. When the cables begin to grind, the harbour lights go off, leaving us in darkness. And the funicular climbs the mountain like a cluster of jewels.

All the way up to the villa the next afternoon, I tell myself that I, too, am clever. I am too clever by half, my mother said, too clever for my own good, said Sister Benedict. But the closer I come to the top of the mountain, the stupider I feel for coming back. I stop just under the verge of the last rise, and wait for my pride to settle. But it won't, it can't. I want to run down again to the blind woman's house and stay there forever just to punish him.

But what would be the point? And what would happen to my children if I did? If the blind woman is right, he would let me wait there until I was old, until my children were grown up and he had corrupted them, too. And then one day he might come for me, or he might not. I sink back against the hill and look out over the sea. It is deadly in the heat, stretching between me and everywhere in the world. And I hate it all completely.

When I climb over the last rise, I stop at the sight of the villa. It is in shadow now, the shutters closed against the heat. He could be watching for me behind them. Or he could be sitting in his chair, not watching at all. I look back at the village. I left the blind woman's house after lunch, as she suggested, when the village people were asleep. Even so, she said, some-

one would know, someone would send word that I was coming back. I feel for the key in my pocket and walk along the
fence to the hidden gate.

And then I see the chain. It is heavy and thick and secured
around the post with an enormous black padlock. Perhaps he
put it there as a joke, a reminder. But I never need reminding. I
am never far from the sound of my mother's screams.

I walk back to the main gates and ring the bell. They swing
open immediately and I walk through, down the long stretch
of driveway to the front door. The garden is silent, no one is
out, not even the rabbits. There is only the smell of the grass
and rotting orangefruit, the stale water of the fountain. When I
reach the front door, it opens. One of the sisters is standing
there, holding it wide. She doesn't look at me, they never look
at me. She just holds the door while I walk into the hall.

"Thea." He stands in the study doorway, looking at me. His
eyes are tired and old and sad. I can see this now because I am
sad myself. I am sad because life is sad, whatever my mother
would say. But still I don't understand how I can hate him for
the blind woman and yet stand here as I do, staring down at the
hands that have been on her blind face and want them on my
own. I want this even though the thought of him and the blind
woman together is making it hard to breathe with the hatred I
have for him, for him led by my father to his own blind daughter, like a dog on a leash.

"You are worse than a dog," I say. "A dog is a king compared
to you."

He sighs as I knew he would. "Come in, Thea," he says. He
loves saying my name, he says it all the time. The nuns loved it,
too. Theadora, Theadora. But my mother never uses it unless

she has to introduce me. And even then, she says, "And this is my daughter." Only if she has to, does she add "Theadora."

"Come in," he says, "there is something I must tell you."

I go to stand behind his leather chair, fixing my eyes on the photograph of him and my father. My father's smile is frightening, with his neat moustache and muscled arm resting on his rifle. How could I not have seen this before? Smiling like that, he could shoot anything with that rifle, me included. If he could have snatched me from my mother sooner, what would he have done with me? Handed me over to the first man who won a bet from him? Any sailor or merchant or thief?

"Here," says Naim, handing me a large leather box. "Sit down before you open it."

I take the box and sit, and close my eyes. I wish that I knew nothing that I know now, and could curl up outside his study door again — a girl wanting only normal happiness. I long for this even though I know it is a hopeless thing to want. And that there is no such thing as normal happiness. Not for me, not ever.

"I have to presume that they are all there," he says. "They are unopened, as you can see."

I look into the box. It is full of letters, neatly stacked. I lift one out. My mother's name, our address, my handwriting. I look up at him. Did she send them back? Unopened? She could have done that, she could be that cruel. If she wants to punish someone, she can be the Queen of Cruelty.

"Sonja took them from the mail bag," he says. "I won't make excuses for her. But you might consider what she has had to give up." He takes the chair opposite and rests his chin on his fingertips. "You must know by now what that is, Thea."

I lift one of the letters and look at her name. "Natalia." When

I write it, I hear her at the piano, talking to herself — "Once more, Natalia," "Good, Natalia." Theadora and Natalia — I used to practise writing the names over and over and over.

He reaches over to me, but I shrink back into the chair, holding the box to my chest.

"Thea —"

"Don't use my name! It is filthy in your mouth! *You* are filthy! You are *worse* than a dog!"

"Thea," he says softly, "don't be like other women. Please. You never have been until now."

"I *am* like other women!" I shout. "I am like every other woman on *earth!*"

But even as I shout this, I know that it can never be true. I am as crippled as the blind woman is blind. I am crippled because my mother is crippled. It is there like the size of my feet, the shape of my eyes. If I weren't crippled, he would not have chosen me. He is a man who chooses his own ugly sister, and a blind woman, and a girl who has been locked up all her life.

"Your notebooks are underneath," he says.

I fling the letters at him, all over the floor, and lift out a diary and throw that too. I don't need to count the months of terrible silence that she has suffered. They are as old as the children, as long as Sonja has been in the house. My own silence is nothing to this — one telegram and the sound of her screams along the docks. What are these to the years she spent lying in the dark, waiting and listening? And how much longer must I be punished by that silence myself?

"Thea —" He stands up, comes over to put his hands on my shoulders. "When I saw you that first afternoon, I saw everything I had lost when I lost my mother. *That* is the truth that you are always wanting so badly."

I look away. I am sinking under the touch of a dog, and I don't want to see his face. My mother always said that, after the War, nothing surprises her. Would it surprise her now that it is his mother I am jealous of? I am jealous of her and I am jealous of myself as I was that first moment when he saw me on the verandah. That is the moment I want back — when I was his and I was my mother's, and I didn't have to choose between them.

"From now on, bring your letters to me," he says. "I will see that she gets them." He lifts my face so that I can see he isn't lying.

I look, but I know that he never lies, he never needs to lie. He is dark and sad in the gloom. Even in the photograph, there is a sort of sadness in his smile, I can see that now.

"Your mother is back in the house," he says. "I am sending you home to her."

I stare at up at him. Home. The word has always felt like a trick, a lie. When I turned the corner with Maude, I could never bear to see it looming there over the jacarandas. And so I would keep my head down as we climbed the hill. Until the padlock clicked shut behind me and the dogs came leaping — until I saw my mother at the door of the lounge with her arms held out to me, home was nothing to me. It was an idea. It was impossible.

"Just me?" I ask. I can hardly force the words out over the terror that has suddenly seized me.

"The children will stay here," he says. "I must be sure that you will return to me, you see."

I stare into the suitcase, trying to remember how Maude used to pack — first one dress, then another, folding them over each other to stop the creases. I love to watch her hands. They are freckled and strong and they smell of the kitchen. When she rolled out pastry, she would dip them into the flour so that they looked like ghosts. "What you watching?" she would ask. "You want some work to do?"

Every night, I have been waking out of the same nightmare. It is that I have been home already, and I am back here. But I remember nothing, not even Maude, not even my mother. I cry in the dream, I beg Naim to send me again. I promise that I will remember everything this time. But he can't seem to hear me. He can't seem to see me either.

He has told me that, while I am gone, Sonja will have the children. Already, in the weeks I have been away, they have forgotten me. At first, when I picked them up, they struggled and cried out to her. But now they hold up their arms to me and smile, and I dance them around. Naim watches all this from his study window, knowing that soon I will be leaving and Sonja will have them back again. Perhaps that is why he made her sit in the corner of my room, watching me when they were born. Every time I think of them, I will have to think of her sitting there in the shadows.

Tomorrow, he will take me down to the boat himself. I know that the blind woman will be there on her balcony, listening as I leave. When he has seen me off, he may even go to her. But I don't care about that anymore. Every night, I lie in the dark thinking of my mother waiting for me at the airport fence, with her scarf tied under her chin. And then of Sonja with my children. And of Naim himself.

He is running his bath. I open the door and climb the stairs, waiting on the landing.

"Come in, Thea," he says.

And so I go in and sit on the ledge. He reaches back for my feet and pulls my legs around his neck so that he can rest his head between my thighs. Tonight we had oysters and a bottle of champagne, and there was a small box in my place, all wrapped and tied with a bow. Inside was a gold locket in the shape of a shell, and inside that, tiny photographs of Nema and Mina. He reached over to show me how to open it even further. And there, right under Nema's picture, was the one of him in Tanganyika, just his dark face, his sad smile.

I close my eyes and lay my head over his. It doesn't seem to matter what he is or how much I have hated him. There is an ache across my heart for him now, too; I can't help it. I am leaving him to go home to my mother, and how could I want it any other way?

Part Three

❧ 1 ❧

The girl has always glistened like a sea animal in the hot season. As soon as they are in the car, she flings off her sandals and stretches her bare feet against the windscreen. "Ma," she sighs. "Oh, Ma, you've gone all grey!"

The gulf of years between them has been like winter itself. When Nalia saw her coming down the steps of the plane with a beaver coat over her arm and earrings swinging through her ears like a native girl, she could find no words with which to scold her, to take her back to herself. So she stood at the fence waiting, shivering despite the heat.

But now, with the girl's bare feet on the windscreen again, and the silence they always keep when they are happy — now Nalia says, "Look! Look there's the house!"

The girl closes her eyes. "*Tell* me what it looks like," she says. "Describe it."

Nalia smiles. How could she have forgotten this? The way the language has always been used between them as a life apart? "Coming up the last rise now," she says, "under the canopy of jacaranda. The house is a gleaming white castle. It is perfect. You can look now."

The girl leaps from the car, still barefoot. She flies down to the gate. The dogs are there already, the gardenboy is running along the path. But then he unlatches the gate and walks through it like a ghost. "The gate's unlocked!" she cries back to Nalia.

"Oh, the gate!" says Nalia, walking through it herself. "Did you see the palms? The elephant creeper had to come down because of rats. The Corporation came around with a paper."

The girl looks up at the naked trees, and then at the house itself, brilliant in the afternoon sun. A strange woman is standing at the front door, smiling. "Where's Maude?" the girl asks Nalia.

But Nalia is making her way along the crazy paving. "We belong where we are born," she is saying. "Elephant ears and palm trees are nothing to me. Nothing at all."

There is refusal in everything about the girl now — the set of her jaw, the steady gaze she keeps just over Vi's head, over the verandah wall and out to sea. As a child, she had begged for cakes from Anglo Swiss, but now she pushes the damp, sweet stuff around with her fork and then sets it aside uneaten. She is jealous, of course, any fool could have seen that coming. But if she had not run off in the first place, if she had come home last year with the babies as Nalia told her to, none of this would have happened.

"Is Maude off today?" she asks Nalia casually.

Nalia lifts her nose like a knife.

"I'll boil some more hot water, Natalia," Vi says quickly.

"Sit down. The tea is hot enough." Nalia turns to the girl. "Everything I have given Maude she has thrown away," she says.

"But *why? How?*"

"Married a taxi driver and went to live in Wentworth." She is about to say more when she sees the girl staring ahead like a blind woman, tears starting in her eyes.

Nalia has never given in to tears, she despises them, but now the sight brings back the whole stretch of time that has passed between them, the stretches that lie ahead. If Vi were not here, she would reach for the girl's hand. She would tell her how she misses Maude herself, the terrible changes in everything, now that they both have gone.

But the girl has turned away. She is fumbling with her necklace, trying to unfasten it. And then, when she has it off, she struggles with the locket, this way and that way, until it opens. "Here," she says, thrusting it at Nalia like a dare. "These are my children. Mina. Nema."

Were Vi not here, Nalia would slap the necklace out of her hand. "'Here'?" she would shout, "What do mean 'here' like that?" But with Vi looking from one to the other like a canary in a cage, they have lost their pitch, their tone, everything that was there between them so naturally before.

Nalia stares at the circled faces in the locket — one serious, one smiling — the miniature gold hoops through their ears. Until now, these children have been like a blot at the edge of a dream, vague beyond imagining. But here they are now, solid and strange and frightening.

"I'll clear the tea things," Vi says.

Nalia watches as she clatters the dishes onto the tray, carrying it with difficulty into the dining room. Despite her size, Vi is as clumsy as a man. Already she has broken a vase and spilled coffee all over the house. Nalia has tried to forbid her coffee anywhere but at a table, but the woman won't work without it. She can't exist without coffee, she says. More than this, she is as obstinate as a mule. Despite Nalia's orders, she lets the dogs onto her bed whenever she feels like it, and she feeds them scraps from the table, too.

Nalia looks again at the locket. The sight of those children, frozen in silence, carries her back, somehow, to her own long years of silence, the way she had to force her thoughts away from a future, any future. "I wish I could see them," she says.

With this, the girl leaps from her chair, and comes to embrace her at last. She wraps her arms around her like a cloak, kissing her cheek, crying openly now, sobbing into her neck.

Nalia has always understood the danger in such happiness. She understands it now, but the girl will not loosen her grip. She lays her head on Nalia's shoulder, and the familiar weight of it, the softness of her hair works on Nalia like sleep. She closes her eyes and rests her cheek on the girl's hair. She has seen the girl herself relax into sleep by a change of mood like this. She has seen her curl up on her lap, quite still, before the talking was even over.

"You'll see Maude tomorrow," she says. "She comes in Monday to Friday like a worker in an office."

"But she's married!" the girl murmurs. "Oh, Ma!"

"Everything changes," Nalia says. But she knows, and so does the girl, that she believes no such thing. All her life she has set herself up against change — against God Himself. And now this is to be her punishment — the girl slipping in and out of her life as she pleases, Maude, too. Perhaps her own mother was right. Perhaps all Nalia's fury was only the fury of helplessness. And even so, how can she help herself? What can she do about it now?

Katzenbogen would simply ask her to tell him again how the fury would start — the buzzing in her head, the way it would roar into her blood, deafening and blinding her to anything but the thing she wanted, the thing she could not have. Scream if you like, he would say. Scream as loud as you like.

But what good is screaming to no purpose? Nothing can change the fact that life takes its own course, whatever you do to contain it. "Give her the rifle," her grandmother would say, "Let her shoot the lot of us and see what it brings her."

❧ 2 ❧

The rule is this: I am to pretend that my other life does not exist. And yet, pretending, it seems to be true. When I sit in the kitchen talking to Maude, it is as if I am making it up, even the children.

"Terrible, that's terrible," she says, shaking salt into the soup. I watch her wedding ring flash, so unfamiliar on her hand that it enchants me.

"He lived with his half-sister like a wife," I say.

She turns to me then, the salt still in her hand. "You telling me lies?" Maude always asks this, even though she has perfect pitch herself for the truth. "She is my eyes and ears," my mother would say. "Don't think you can get around her."

And so I tell her about the nurses, and the blind woman, and the man who spat on me in the village. Now that she is married, I can tell her anything I like, even about Nema, what happened with the waiter on the ship.

She gives up the soup then and comes to stand at the table. It is spread with newspaper so that she can gut and clean the fish we are having for dinner. The whole kitchen smells happily of fish. It smells of Fridays, home from school.

"You telling me lies?" she says again, her eyes muddy, dark and frightening. If my children were here, I would hold them to me, turning their faces from her. I have seen her cross the kitchen to scold the gardenboy with her eyes like this, and the chopping knife still in her hand. Even when she has put it down, he still stares at it. Maude can make anything happen if she is angry enough. She can make a knife lift itself through the air and back into her hand.

"You must tell your father to bring the children here," she says.

I laugh. "My father! He's the worst of all!"

She clicks her tongue. When I sound like my mother, she has nothing to say, and I wish now that I hadn't told her anything. How would she ever understand that the truth is not so simple? That even now, telling her about Naim, there is something I can hardly understand myself. It is that I long for him. All those months before the children, when he waited for me every day in his study, every evening at the dining room table — I want them back. When I remember him like this, I am hardly a mother at all.

"When can I meet your husband?" I ask. Her hands are at the fish, bloodied and strong. It is impossible to think of them touching a man, absolutely impossible.

"He can't come here," she says.

"Then I'll come to Wentworth. They won't even notice that I'm gone."

She looks up to see if I am joking. But we both know that my mother has taken to Vi like a lover. If she doesn't lock her up in the way she did me, it is only because she doesn't need to.

Every morning, they make their way down through the rockery to the summerhouse, and there they take off their dressing gowns and face into the sun, naked. They breathe and stretch and bend, and I stand on the upstairs verandah, watching them the way I watched my own children. And the strange thing is that, down there, they seem like children themselves. Without clothes, even their bodies are childlike. And they squabble and fight. Once I saw my mother throw Vi's dressing gown over the fence into Mrs. Holmes's garden. And then Vi had to follow my mother up the rockery, right past the gardenboy, quite naked.

"Maybe Sonny can fetch you on Sunday," Maude says. She doesn't look at me. She is filleting the fish, one flash of the knife, and then, slap, the other side.

It is a mad idea, we both know this. How would it happen? Maude's husband ringing the gate bell and me walking through it, shouting goodbye? Even though the padlock is gone, no one except Maude comes through that gate without ringing the bell. Vi herself goes out only if my mother takes her. If my mother leaves without her, she lies on the verandah swing seat with the dogs around her feet, waiting for her to return.

"What time should I be ready?" I say to Maude, my heart galloping.

"Quarter past twelve. After church comes out."

❧ 3 ❧

Nalia wakes every morning like a warrior waiting for dawn. First the calisthenics. Then breakfast. Then, at nine o' clock, Vi shuts the doors and they start practising. If Nalia had her way, they would start even earlier, but Vi will not hear of it. She has to grind her beans and drink her coffee. Nalia will not let her use Maude for this. If Vi is going to keep her waiting, she is also going to know whose house this is, and who, between them, has never ruined her life over a man.

But then, at the piano, Vi is hard and sharp and true. "Lyric soprano?" she cries. "You're no lyric soprano! Now take it again from 23, please. Hit the floor!"

Closed in with Vi, Nalia is as happy as she can remember. Of all the things missing since the War, this has been the most forgotten to her. And even if it is too late for her voice to be what it might have been — still, when she is singing for Vi, she is full of hope again. It doesn't even matter that Vi is only here because her own life is over, that when she is not at the piano, she is a flatterer and a wheedler and a fool. It was providence that sent the woman to Nalia that first afternoon in the mountains — to make sense of this house again, and of her life in it.

Even on a Sunday, like today, Nalia insists on two hours of practising before they do anything else. She knows that Vi can't find a way to tell her that she wants a day off. A day off for what? A trip up the coast? Tea at the hotel?

"There's a note for you on the kist, Natalia," Vi says, as soon as the practising is over. She has not yet learned that she is never to read Nalia's mail, not even the addresses on the envelopes. "Here," she says, "looks as if it's from Theadora."

Nalia snatches the note from her hand. She puts on her glasses and stares at the name written on the outside. "Natalia." The girl has always loved writing their names in her bold, loose hand. *Natalia and Theadora.* Nalia and the girl, Nalia and her own grandmother.

"Anything wrong?" Vi asks.

The woman is always asking this, concerned that she might be thrown out by the same chance that brought her into this house in the first place. At the same time, she is always hoping, always scrutinising the kist for something with her own name on it, jumping up like a girl when the phone rings. When Nalia mocks her, she only grows pathetic, repulsive, grotesque. "What I *cannot* believe," she cries, "is that I will never make love to a man again!"

"Ma, I've gone to Maude's for lunch. I'll be back at about five. Thea."

Nalia folds the note and starts up the stairs. But then, on the first landing, she has to stop for a moment. A knife has suddenly been slipped under her ribs, almost stopping her breathing.

"Anything wrong?" Vi calls out again.

"Find some lunch for yourself in the fridge," Nalia says. "I'm not hungry."

She pulls herself up, one stair at a time, right up to the top, and then along the passage and into her room, locking the door behind her. She falls across the bed without taking off the spread, without even undressing. The curtains are huffing in the afternoon breeze. Native boys are strumming along the pavement, and Sunday afternoon planes are out for a flip.

Everything seems more normal than ever. So why does it matter so much that the girl went off without even asking? If she had never left in the first place — if she, Nalia, had the girl's future back in her own hands, what would she want for it? The answer is, Nothing. Until the thief came and snatched her away, there was nothing of the future between Nalia and the girl — only the day, the hour, everything stretched into one long line.

Nalia curls onto her side to ease the pain. On Tuesday, when she goes inland, she won't read Katzenbogen her notebook after all. She will ask him what was so terrible about the girl and her growing older together in one long line? She will ask him if it was vanity after all to want to keep the girl for herself as she did, as she does.

He won't answer, of course. She will have to wait until later, when he unlaces his shoes and places them on the floor, perfectly polished, perfectly straight. Then he will stretch himself out on the bed in the little room, and he will say what he always says — that for Nalia, the girl has always been the flesh and echo of herself — her furious persistence, her pride, her revenge. She will watch him as he tells her this and, somehow, for a moment, she will understand. She will sit against the footboard of the bed, with the smell of Knight's Castile and Cobra polish — and, oh, Nalia longs for his hand in her life again.

❧ 4 ❧

Maude is waiting in an apron when Sonny and I arrive. She takes the jar of Maraschino cherries I have brought her from the pantry and gives it to Sonny. "Thanks," she says.

I know she will take it back to the house tomorrow. If my mother missed it, she would know where it went and why. Maude takes my hand in hers and leads me up the hill to her kitchen door.

"This is my dog," she says. "This is the back door, sorry." She smells of onions and Wild Gardenia, and I wish with all my heart that we were all home again together.

"Mummy," Sonny calls out, "must I open the Fanta?"

"Open the Coke," she says. "You still like Coke, hey?"

I nod. There is no voice, no language between us for this new life of hers. She leads me down the main passage of the house, still holding my hand. "There's the lav, in case you have to go," she says. She stops in the doorway of her bedroom, where I am to leave my bag. There are two beds side by side, neatly made up with white crocheted bedspreads. And there are nylon voiles on the windows, and a set of doilies under the glass of the dressing table. But no candles, no statue of the Virgin Mary.

"Lunch is ready," she says. "It mustn't get cold."

At the table, she bows her head for Sonny to say grace. If she were not married, I would beg her to come back to the island with me. She would stay in the room next to mine, and Sonja would never dare to come down the passage again, she would never dare to touch my children, either.

"Maude cooks better than a hotel," Sonny says. He is much darker than Maude, and his bald head glistens with sweat. "She could do catering for people in town."

I flush at the thought of my mother, innocent of all this. All the way out of town and onto the airport road, Sonny was silent at the wheel, never turning to me. But now he stares at me with his small yellow eyes. He is about to say something more when Maude says, "Cut some bread, please."

He grips the loaf and saws at it fiercely. His fingers are spidery, and the flesh under his fingernails is purple. Turning away, I try to remember Naim's hands, Naim himself. Lying in bed at night, I open my locket to his photograph and hold it up to the lamp. But he is lost to me here, he is a shadow. Even the children are frozen into those small circled faces. As long as I am here, my life on the island could be a dream. It could be nothing.

"She made this bread, too," Sonny says, pushing the breadboard towards her.

"Hau, what's wrong with you, showing off?" Maude says, trying to laugh it off.

I try to laugh, too. All though lunch, I praise the biryani she has made specially for me, the mango chutney, the fingerbowls at each place, just like ours. But she is shy in her own house, nothing like herself. She just says, "Same old recipe we always had. Want some more?"

I shake my head.

"No wonder you skinny as a dog," Sonny says.

I smile, but he is cleaning something out of his teeth now with the fork and he won't look at me.

Maude stretches her hand across to touch his arm. "Hey!" she says. She stands and begins to clear the plates. I stand, too, but she says, "I'm just bringing the trifle. Wait there."

The house is hot in the afternoon sun. Down the hill and across the valley are hundreds of little houses like this, with red dirt roads cutting in among them. How can Maude be herself in this new life? It is almost as strange as my own.

"You still like trifle?" she says, spooning a huge helping into a bowl.

"Why you forcing her, woman? Can't you see she doesn't like our food."

Maude sits back at last, staring at him with her old, fierce eyes.

"I'm trying to teach her, that's all," he says to me. "She's been cooking all last night and this morning. I told her, after the baby she's got to take it easy."

I put down my spoon. "Maude?"

But she has pushed herself to her feet. She has the salt cellar in her hand and would throw it at him, I know, if she could bear to break it. "What did I tell you?" she says. "Didn't I *tell* you not to say?"

He smiles, trying to take her free hand in both of his. But she pulls it back and moves beyond his reach. "Why can't you keep your mouth closed when someone asks you? What's wrong with you, hey? You want to hurt people that have never hurt you?"

He is up now, too, holding on to the back of the chair. "What you talking about? *Who* never hurt me? Every morning I must drive you to that woman, and every night I must fetch you there myself!"

Maude pulls a hanky out of her pocket and blows her nose. "Don't you be sad," she says to me.

"Why should *she* be sad?" Sonny shouts, pointing a finger at me. "Who is she to be sad? Your own daughter?"

Maude shakes her head. "Ai," she says, "you always making trouble."

I have never seen her cry. I have only seen her cross or happy, except that even when she's happy, she seems cross. But she is crying now — furiously, silently, still staring at him.

"She's got her *own* mother!" he shouts at her. He pushes past her, out of the room, slamming a door down the passage.

She comes around the table to me then. "Don't worry about him," she says softly. "Sometimes he can be nice."

I lean against her, clasping my arms around her hips. "Oh Maude!" I say. "But it's *lovely* about the baby!"

She combs my hair back from my forehead with her fingers. "If it's a girl, I'll call her Thea," she says. "I told him that already. Every night, I pray to the Lord for a girl."

5

I asked my father to arrange driving lessons for me because my mother is ill. For six days now, she has been in bed, curled around a hot water bottle. If I come in, she pretends to be asleep. She has always taken illness as an affront. I am not to ask, I am not to know, either.

All the way down the hill, my father is triumphant. "What ho, hey?" he says, grinning. "You're dressed for a garden party, I see."

I flush. I have put on my American dress and a pair of high-heeled sandals, painted my toenails with my mother's varnish, and twisted my hair into a chignon so that the earrings can be seen. I don't even consider what I will tell her about this. Since I came home, I have forgotten all my old ways of lying to her. And anyway, she hardly seems to care, she hardly seems to notice me anymore.

"Naim bought me this dress," I say.

He laughs. "Good for him! After the driving lesson, I'll take you to tea at the Balmoral to show you off."

The driving teacher lights a cigarette, holding it to his lips between thumb and forefinger. He has long hair and his shirt-sleeves are rolled up over his muscles. "I like shy girls," he says.

I stare ahead at a tug docked at the end of the pier. For an hour, we have stayed in the parking lot, stopping and starting. When I walked into the driving school office and he looked up from his desk, running his eyes along the neckline of my dress with his cocky smile, the blood beat into my face and neck and ears, and I have been silent ever since.

"By the way, I'm Dirk," he says. We have come to a stop outside his office with the engine still running. The driving school itself is nothing more than this shack down in the yacht basin parking lot. He fixes cars, too, he says. If my mother needs her car fixed, she can bring it to him.

"Want to go for a walk? Down the pier?"

I shrug.

"Then you can walk me back to my office." He laughs as if he has cracked a joke. "Come on," he says, "don't be shy." He turns off the car and gets out.

As we walk down the pier, he keeps his hand on my elbow. "Hey!" he shouts. Two men are hanging over the railing of the tug, watching us approach. "Look what I brought you!"

I try to smile, but with all of them looking at me, I wish I had worn an ordinary sundress and flat shoes. And yet this is what I dressed up for this morning — men looking at me, men wanting me for themselves. I didn't even want to learn to drive as much as I wanted this. For all I know, it is why Naim bought me the clothes in the first place. For all I know, it is why he sent me home.

"The old man's daughter," Dirk shouts, pointing to my father's launch.

"Has he got any more for us?"

They laugh, and I laugh with them. And then, somehow, laughing, I find something to say. "I am married," I say to Dirk.

He stops and stares at me. "You joking!"

"No. I am, really."

He takes his hand from my elbow. "Stole you from the cradle then, hey?"

"Sort of."

We walk back to my father's car in silence, as if we have had a fight. He reaches in through the window and presses the hooter, which my father has told him to do.

"Your old man will take over now," he says. "Cheers!"

My father and I sit on the verandah of the Balmoral, looking out over the beachfront. I have seen him sullen like this when my mother announces before coffee that the evening is over. Or when she concentrates on her embroidery and pretends not to hear what he is saying.

"What's given your mother the vapours?" he says.

"Dr. Slatkin's coming on his way home."

He pulls out his pocket watch. "Drink up," he says, "Maybe I'll pop in to see her."

But I am so full of longing, so full of regret that I don't even hear what he has said. "Why did you let Naim win me in a bet?" I blurt out.

He calls the waiter over. "You're happy enough," he says.

"I am *not!* I am *not* happy!" Tears of self-pity fill my eyes.

"Too late for all that. Come on, my girl, time to go."

I follow him out of the hotel. All these years, I have watched my mother hating him, and I have only used her hatred to amuse him myself. But now I want to punish him. I want him to know that I cannot even have a driving lesson like a normal girl. I am a cripple not just because she is a cripple. I am a cripple because he has crippled me, too.

"You have ruined my life!" I scream at him. We are on the steps of the hotel, and I don't care if people are staring, I want them to stare. "He sold me like a slave!" I shout at them.

He grabs my arm. "Stop it at once!" he growls. People turn to watch him march me to the car. I am crying loudly now, as loudly as I can. "Jesus Christ!" he shouts. "What are you up to, shrieking like a fishwife?" He opens the door and pushes me in.

All the way through the racecourse and up the hill, I turn away from him, heaving and shuddering. When we come to the final rise, I don't even look away from the house. I stare right at it. It is huge and frightening in the afternoon sun.

He stops in the driveway. "Get a grip on yourself before we go in," he says. He reaches into his pocket and pulls out some money. "Here. Busfare and so forth. You can find your own way down there on Tuesday."

I ignore the money and open the door, slam it closed again.

"Just like your bloody mother," he shouts, jumping out, too, and following me closely, before I can close the gate. "It's a bloody shame!"

I watch them from the shadow of the upstairs verandah — the extraordinary sight of him standing next to my mother's bed. He has captured both her wrists with his left hand and is feeling her forehead with his right.

"All right," he says, letting her go, "I'm going to send my own doctor up. Just instruct that creeping Jesus downstairs to let him in when he comes."

She turns her back to him and pulls the covers right up around her neck. "*Vi!*" she screeches. "*Vi!* Come here at once!"

"Oh, do shut up, you know she can't hear you." He goes to sit in her green chair and crosses his legs, crosses his arms as well. But he keeps staring at the mound she has made of herself in the bed, he lifts his chin to sniff at the air like a dog. "Maude should be here," he says at last. "That creeping Jesus is too old. And Theadora has no common sense."

"Who's fault is that?"

I flush hot with rage. If I knew she would take my side, I would burst into the room. But she is lying there talking to him. He is sitting in her chair and she isn't even reaching for the bell.

"Natalia," he says, "what is all this about? Are you really ill?"

She turns onto her back and stares up at the ceiling. "I should go back to the mountains," she says. "I was happy there."

I know she means to punish him with this, but I am the one who is punished. Why should he care if she goes to the mountains? What is she to him except through me?

"Ah well," he says, slapping his hands onto his knees and standing up. "I'd suggest you do something with that hair of yours before you go. It doesn't become you to be an old woman."

6

After all, it comes in words — the plunder, the ravishment, the desolation. These are not the words that Slatkin uses, of course. He sits behind his desk with his pale fingers knitted in front of him and says, "Nalia, my old friend, this is not good news."

All this Nalia will repeat to Katzenbogen with a laugh. Driving up, she will roll down the windows and sing however she pleases, to hell with Vi. Next week, perhaps, she'll send Vi back to the mountains, so that she and the girl can have the house to themselves again.

The girl is stretched out on the divan. She has always been like a dog when the suitcases come down — sober, miserable, hopeless. "Ma," she says, "why can't I go with you for once?"

Her hands are still dimpled, like a child's. And yet, day after day, off she goes on the bus to her driving lesson, as if she will grow older by driving. When Nalia looks at the girl's hands, she wants to cry for the sadness of life itself. "Ring down to Maude, darling," she says. "Ask her to come up and pack before she has her tea."

Nalia sighs. When death was everywhere around her — savage, vicious, fickle — it was nothing like this. Even when the girl was snatched away and Nalia thought she wanted to die right then, what had she wanted but a punishment? A lie? Death is nothing like that. It is a gift, it is a blessing. Katzenbogen will say that she is enjoying herself with this idea, and perhaps he will be right this time. All her life Nalia has wanted to be sure. And now here it is — this surprise, this clean, plain truth.

The girl slumps back down. "Maude's coming," she says.

Nalia can see that she is close to tears. If she could bear to part with the truth, she would give it to her now. But she can't, not yet. First, she will tell Katzenbogen. She is mad to tell Katzenbogen. "Hurry up," she says to Maude. "I'm late already."

Maude holds up the green knit dress and jacket. "Not too hot for this?"

"There's still snow on the mountains."

"Okay. What about shoes? Black or beige?" Maude takes out both pairs and holds them to the dress, looking from Nalia to the girl. Something is wrong with both of them these days, she thinks. Nalia is quiet and calm, and the girl is like a cat, all over the place, waiting for the phone to ring. When Maude asks who is phoning, the girl only gets cheeky, telling her to mind her own beeswax.

"The beige ones," says the girl.

"All right," Nalia says, "put them in." She looks at her watch. "I must be on the road pronto."

"Ma? Why did you cut off your hair like that?"

Nalia comes to sit on the divan. "What's the matter with you today, darling?" Her voice is soft, as it always is when she's going inland. She smooths the girl's hair off her forehead. "Going for a driving lesson today?"

The girl nods, but her lip is quivering. Everything is slipping away — her mother, her children, Maude, Naim. No word has come from him, no letters, nothing. When she asked her father about him, he only said, "Trees fall all over the forest, my dear."

"On Thursday, perhaps we'll go up the coast," Nalia says. "You can drive, you'll have your licence by then. What about that?"

The girl looks up at the familiar creases around her mother's mouth, the halo of grey hair catching the morning light. "I never read you my diaries anymore," she says.

"When I come back? Promise?"

"But Vi is always here."

Nalia smiles. How many times did the girl use all her wiles to hold Nalia back from leaving? And then, at last, she would sit up on the sleeping porch, banging on the glass. She lifts the girl's hand and kisses the dimples, all in a row. The skin is sleek and soft and she holds it to her cheek. Nothing Nalia can do can change what will happen now. But suddenly her heart aches at the thought of this girl left behind. Except for death, there are no mistakes in life? What on earth had Katzenbogen meant by that? Death is no mistake. It was there all along, Slatkin says, years of it hidden away. Well now, here it is, and not even Katzenbogen can think up words to change that.

"I must be off," she says. "You know where to find me."

The girl closes her eyes and listens for the slam of the front door, and then of the gate, and then of the garage itself. Already Vi is putting on a record. She listens for Nalia's departures as carefully as the girl herself used to. And the dogs shadow her everywhere now for the biscuits she keeps in her pockets. Maude has complained to Nalia of crumbs in Vi's sheets. But Nalia just sighs and says, "I'll be sending her away soon anyway."

Still, Vi stays on. Every morning, they go down to the lower lawn to do their calisthenics together. And the girl watches them from the upstairs verandah. When Nalia goes into the lounge to practise, she slips downstairs and opens the door softly, standing there for a moment just to see her mother's face lifted in all the old happiness. Now that Vi is not coaching her anymore, Nalia sings her old songs in the old way, and sometimes the girl crawls under the piano and stretches out there as she used to. But she feels ridiculous now, lying on the floor, looking at her mother's foot on the pedal. "Happiness?" her mother used to say. "Happiness is a toothless old woman with a bowl of cold porridge to eat."

The girl pads through to her mother's bedroom and slumps onto the bed. The sun is roaring through the open French doors, bringing a cloud of gnats. The room smells of talcum powder and this morning's eggs, and she is as miserable as she ever was on the island.

She is still in her shortie pyjamas. She wears them only to please her mother. Since her first driving lesson, she has put away all the clothes that she brought with her. She wears her old things again, still hanging just where she left them in the wardrobe — the *broderie anglaise,* the green velvet, everything she gambled and squandered for Naim.

She opens the drawer of the bedside table to look for the stopwatch she always loved to play with. But she finds a notebook instead. It is an ordinary black school notebook, and she pulls it out and opens it. The pages are covered with her mother's handwriting. She knows every loop and cross, the way the words string into each other, on and on, with the full stops stabbing through the paper.

She turns to the beginning, scanning page after page for her name. But there is nothing of herself there — only mountains, blue in the morning light, and her grandmother's lover, a lake, a ghost man coming out of the mist. She is reading her mother's life without her in it, a story in which she does not even exist.

"What you doing on the bedspread?" Maude says, standing in the doorway. "Why you reading what doesn't belong to you?"

The girl looks up. "Who is the ghost man?"

"You asking rubbish," Maude says, clicking her tongue. "No ghosts in this world. Only in books."

Riding along the ridge on the top of a bus, the girl stares out of the window at people on the pavement. Once, taking the bus with Maude, she had seen a man lying dead in the road, with a crowd around him. As the bus passed, she saw a boy thrust his hand into the man's pocket and pull out some money. When she told this to Maude, Maude only said, "What does he care now? That's not him anymore. He's gone."

She decides to get off at the Central Post Office and to walk down Commercial Road to the yacht basin. She has never been allowed to walk by herself before, so she stops to look at the fish and chips shop, and the municipal park, the garage where her mother's car is fixed. As she passes, two garage men look up at her and whistle. "Hello!" one shouts. "All grown up now, darling?" He has a cigarette behind his ear like Dirk. He probably smells like Dirk, too. It is the way Naim smells when he comes back from the shipyard, and she loves to think that it is the smell of common rubbish.

She thinks a lot about common rubbish these days, but not in the way she did before. What had scared her then was the way they seemed to know what they wanted, what you wanted yourself. Words were nothing to them. There was only their need, the way it took over the world. To Dirk, she is her father's money and her husband's wife. "What would they say about this?" he likes to ask, laying a hand on her thigh.

She is wearing her old sundress and cork wedges, and her hair is tied back into a ponytail. She has taken the varnish off her toenails and she does not wear lipstick anymore. Only the blind woman's earrings seem alive in the way she was alive herself when she got off the plane. They have a lovely heaviness to them, swinging like the ticking of a clock as she walks.

When she arrives at the yacht basin, Dirk is lying on his back under a car. She stands for a moment in the shade of the shack, watching him. She loves the smell of this place — petrol and fish and the stale salt water of the bay.

She never has to tell him she is here. He is like Naim in this way. Perhaps all men are like this, she thinks, even her father. He often comes out onto the deck of his launch just as her mother is dropping her off. "There he is," her mother says, "sniffing us out like a dog."

Her father's launch is even bigger than Naim's. It has its own lift and a small pool, and she longs to see the inside of it. But he will never allow this. If he allowed her onboard, he says, she would grow fins like all the others, and circle and circle. And then he would never be rid of her, never.

"Early today, hey?" Dirk says, getting up. He wipes his hands on a rag and throws it at the shack. "Ready to go?"

She climbs into her father's car and starts it up, reverses, brings it around to the railway tracks. Her father seems to have forgotten how she shouted at him at the Balmoral, or else he doesn't care. When he fetches her now, he lets her drive herself down for the lesson. "Where are your fancy clothes?" he asks. "The old cow hide them away?"

Dirk just stares out of his window as she manoeuvres them through the traffic, moody, silent. At last he says, "What's going to happen after tomorrow?"

"After tomorrow? Nothing. Why?"

"I mean, if you're going to come down here anymore."

She opens the window to let in the warm air. It is soft and damp and familiar. And yet, with Dirk sitting next to her, the world outside is as strange as the island. Perhaps this is what men can do to the earth, she thinks. They can turn even the things you know into strangers.

"I can stay on late this afternoon if you like," she says. She is deft with the car, parking it with two turns of the wheel. She could have taken her test a week ago, but they decided between them that she would stretch it out as long as possible.

"Okay," he says, "that's it." He walks back to the shack so that she has to follow him. She waits at the door while he touches the lead of a pencil to his tongue and writes down in a thick, dark hand the amount he will charge her father for this lesson.

"You'll pass the test easy tomorrow," he says, looking at his watch. "Want an evening swim?" he says. "We can go in the van."

🐝 7 🐝

Nalia has never been superstitious, Katzenbogen knows that. So he will believe her when she tells him that her dream was more than a dream. For weeks now, Nalia has been remembering things in dreams, hanging them around her like curtains. But this dream was different. It seemed to carry with it a knife at the throat of the girl herself. And then, when she woke up, it had already retreated like a ghost, leaving only this urgency to obey, this terror of consequences.

She knows how it started — with the student from the university, so avid, so greedy to have Nalia's life for herself. When she wound her way around to asking Nalia, as usual, about the girl's father — sitting forward on the rocking chair, holding out the microphone — what did she think Nalia would do this time? Shine a torch around the back of that old story for her? Right into the shadows, into the corners?

But then there it was that night in the dream — the girl chasing after the car, wanting an answer herself, the nonentity sitting in the backseat, silent. Of course, Katzenbogen will want to know how Nalia felt when the nonentity actually came marching into the house, right up to her room, and captured her wrists in his hand. But she will just tell him to shut up and let her dig the truth of the dream out into the light, let her drown the truth in light once and for all.

She parks, as usual, behind the hotel, and leaves her grip with the little man at the desk.

"Welcome," he says. "We was wondering what happened to you."

She signs the book and hands him the money, counted out and ready in the pocket of her jacket. "My usual room, I trust," she says, "my usual table."

She stands for a moment, pretending to check the clasp of her bag, but the smell of fried onions and old floor polish has her faint with longing and regret. She even longs for the lousy wine that Katzenbogen always orders. The first glass will close them instantly into their old silence. She will watch him cut into his monkey-gland steak, his ears turning red from the wine, and she, who has given up the future so many times already, will be waiting, as she is always waiting, somehow, for the next thing to start.

Nalia begins the story with his awful blue suit, a suit made for a man with shoulders, not for Katzenbogen, who sagged in everything he wore, but especially in that suit. When she opened her dressing room door to him that first night, she had not recognised him in that suit, without his beard. She saw only a man who would look at himself in the mirror and see nothing — no past, no future. She would have called in the stagehands to throw him out right then if he hadn't asked quickly, in that soft voice of his, what she thought she was doing, performing Wagner, for God's sake?

And then she knew. And she fell back against the dressing table with a cry.

All this, he knows already. But she will tell him again anyway, because, from now on, he will think of it differently. He will remember asking whether he could touch her again, and then, when she nodded, touching her like a blind man, all ten fingers so lightly on her skin that she had to close her eyes to shut out the sight of him in that suit. May I? he said, and, Is this all right?

Why did he have to ask like that? As if he wanted a dance, or a glass of water? Why does he still ask now? Doesn't he know that asking will tell him nothing about desire? That if she hasn't told him this before, it is because there are no answers to such questions. If he wants an answer, he should have been there when the King of Greed swept her into a dance on the deck of his launch. Oh, he would have seen a different Nalia then!

She laughs. Katzenbogen, who asks her to remember to the farthest reaches of Hell, just sits in silence when she speaks of her first night with the nonentity. Sometimes, he uncaps his pen and writes in his notebook, looking up after a while, right into the face of her old happiness. And when that happiness was snatched away, and she, Nalia, told him that she would stick to the child she was carrying, girl or boy, like a lichen to a gravestone, all he could say then was that it was her own life she was planning to give birth to — the whole story told another way.

She stares up at his bookshelf, the familiar spines so carefully arranged. The room smells of leather and wool, and she could fall asleep right now, before her time is up. "There are only two things I have left out of my notebook," she says at last. "This death, and the girl. There is nothing in there about the girl."

She can hear him move forward to hear what she is saying, but, lying on the couch with her eyes closed, it is as if she is speaking to herself, a madwoman on a bus. She strokes the soft flesh under her arm. The girl used to love to find it there. She would lie with her head in Nalia's lap and reach up to stroke it as if it were her own.

Usually, when she is falling asleep, Katzenbogen finds something to say to bring her back. But now he doesn't speak at all, and she cannot help it, she closes her eyes and drops away from him.

She waits as usual while he finishes his steak, watching the familiar curve of his brow, the small, flat ears moving as he chews. In the barbarous light of their room upstairs, she will take him all in — the head and the hands years older than the rest of him, and then the sallow body itself, surprisingly muscled and smooth.

"You are taking too long," she says. "You always take too long."

He places his knife and fork together immediately, wipes his mouth on his napkin.

But she sits back and picks up the wine menu. "I'll have a cognac," she says.

He holds up his hand for the wine steward. "Two cognacs, please. Rémy Martin."

When the cognac is delivered, she takes her time, cradling the snifter, swilling the liquid around the glass. He is watching her, she knows, waiting for the thing she came all the way inland to say. But he will not ask. They could sit down here all night, and he would never ask her to tell him what she does not choose to.

Nalia has never found an answer to the way a man can love her like this. Nor to her own desire — how, when she closes her eyes to him in the room upstairs, it is always Katzenbogen and a woman, any woman at all, pushed against his leather couch, or on the bend of the hotel stairs, or even her own assistant over the chair in her dressing room that first night all those years ago.

"I cannot bear to leave her to that thief," she says to him at last.

"You have a choice?" He sits back and folds his arms.

"I will write it all in my notebook for her," she says. "I will rip her from his hard, cold eyes."

Suddenly, he reaches across the table to grasp her wrist, knocking her cognac over. "Go away!" he shouts at the waiter. "Leave it! Nalia!" he says. "I want to hear it now."

She looks away. She knew how this would be, even the words he would utter, this desperate voice. But the thought of the girl looking for herself in this face, these hands, is unbearable now.

"Nalia! For God's sake! Tell me!"

She shakes her head. She can't do it after all. When Katzenbogen used to ask her to remember what the girl had said, what she had said to the girl herself, she could never do it then, either. It was like a part she had sung and long forgotten. And now, here he is again, urgent, insistent — "Nalia, I *have* to know! I have a *right* to know!"

But if she tells him, her whole life will be told another way. And everyone will be punished. Everyone.

"You don't need to say it," he says. "Just let me say it for you. I am her father — that is it, isn't it? That is what you came to tell me today?"

She closes her eyes. She does not want to see him watching her cry. "Yes," she says. "Yes."

❦ 8 ❦

"Want another lager before we swim?" Dirk says, opening a bottle with his teeth. The sand is still warm, the wind, too. But the surf is up, wild and thundering along the beach.

"I used to come down to the river on Sunday mornings with my mother," she says.

"Well, you're grown up now, hey?" He reaches for the zip of her sundress and pulls it down.

She stands to let it fall to the sand. And then she slips off her pants, turning so that he can see her in the fading light. Until now, they have been hidden from each other in the darkness at the back of his van, but today she wants him to have the whole sight of her, everything she sees for herself in the mirror.

"Swim first," he says, taking off his own clothes.

She knows he wants to terrify her with the water. All these weeks he has been waiting for her to agree to an evening swim, and now here he is, slim and smooth, nothing like Naim. He takes her hand and pulls her down the steep bank of sand to the water.

"Hold on to my shoulders and hold your breath," he says.

She links her arms around his neck and flattens herself over him, closing her eyes against the terror of the water — breathing it in, choking and coughing as he dives under wave after wave. And then, just as she thinks she will give up, just as she loosens her grip and is trying to say, "I am going back in," they reach the smooth waters beyond the breakers.

"See?" he says, clasping her from behind, floating with her, treading water.

The water is black as ink and warm. She lays her head back on his shoulder and looks up at the dark sky. It doesn't matter to her who he is or that he seemed to find her by such chance. She knows that it wasn't chance at all. If it had not been Dirk, some other man would have come for her — someone who would have taken her without asking, as her father took her mother. And if Naim takes possession of him in turn, she doesn't care about that either. If she can long for Naim, foul as the Devil, then she can float here with Dirk, forgetting completely about the future.

"Why don't you leave him?" Dirk says. "Why not?"

She stares at the easy glow of his cigarette, his easy life.

"What you need is a real man to take care of you," he says.

She looks out through the darkness at the beams of light moving across the causeway — cars going home for the night. She has always watched normal lives at a distance like this. When she comes too close, they seem to disappear, like the rabbits in the garden of the villa.

"I have children," she says.

"You joking, hey?"

She shakes her head. She is still too happy to care what she says to him. And out here, the children seem like a dream — an idea attached to another life.

"Christ!" he shouts. "What kind of a woman are you?"

"I'm a tart." There is pleasure in the word, after all. If he were not ready to hit her, she would tell him that she loves him. But how would he understand that? How would this furious man, who can't even spell her name properly, understand that she doesn't care what he thinks of her?

He starts the van and roars it out of the parking lot, onto the beach road. When he turns up towards the ridge, she says, "You can stay all night if you like."

"What?" He slows down a bit. "What you talking about now?"

"My mother has gone inland."

"Ha! So when the cat's away, hey?"

She shrugs. She should be in tears by now, but the happiness will not go away. It is a happiness not only for Dirk, but for herself, for Naim — for everything that she will take back with her to the island.

He drives on in silence, through the racecourse and up the hill. "What about the servants?"

"They're gone until tomorrow. There's only my mother's friend there, but she doesn't matter."

He parks the van against the big jacaranda as usual.

"You don't need to put on your shoes," she says, flinging her sandals over her shoulder, and climbing out.

When Vi opens the door, she says, "May I have the keys to the liquor cabinet please, Vi?" She walks past her and into the hall, leaving Dirk to follow.

Vi blinks at Dirk. "Ah!" she cries. "The liquor cabinet! Coming right up!"

"Jeez! What a place!" Dirk stands in the hall, staring around him. "Hey," he says, "there's sand all over the floor."

"So what?" She takes his hand and leads him through the lounge, out onto the verandah. "Look," she says, pointing at the lights of the harbour below them. "That's where we were just now." She puts her arms around his neck and pulls him to her, kissing him hard, holding him there so that he can't help it, he grinds her against the pillar, almost choking her with his tongue.

"Ah, there you are!" Vi cries. She is in the doorway, holding up the key like a bell. "I'll leave it on the table then, shall I? Be upstairs if you need me."

The girl laughs as she leaves. "What do you want to drink?" she asks Dirk. "Whiskey? Brandy?"

"You got brandy and Coke?"

"Come," she says, taking him back inside.

Death comes at its own pace, hiding for days, and then, on the next, making Nalia sick at the smell of an omelette. "Take it away," she says to Maude. "Put it out in the passage."

Maude stands where she is, stalwart with the tray. "You got to eat some breakfast," she says, "I don't care what."

Nalia does not look up from her notebook — writing, crossing out.

"Maybe you shouldn't leave that notebook lying around," Maude says.

"What?"

But Maude presses her lips together. When her baby is born, what will happen to this madwoman then? What will happen to her, stuck at home with a husband and a baby and a dog?

"Bring me the potty, I'm going to be sick."

Maude puts down the tray and runs, but it is too late. Nalia is heaving into the sleeve of her dressing gown, onto the chair.

"Here, stand up." Maude lifts the gown from her. "Now the nightie."

Despite the heat, Nalia is shivering.

"Come," Maude says, leading her through to the bathroom. She runs a basin of warm water. "You getting too thin," she says. "What's the matter with you these days?"

Nalia holds onto the basin, listening to the girl thumping past, down the passage. She comes and goes now as she pleases, asking for the car keys, slamming out through the front door. Once, Nalia would have demanded the name of the man she brought into the house while she was gone. She would have locked her up or thrown her out entirely.

But she is tired now, and the girl has come home with too many secrets. Nalia herself can't even find a way to write down the simple truth. When she searches for the words, she only moves further and further into the things that went before, the things that came afterwards. How else can she make the girl understand that Katzenbogen was an accident of Fate? And that if she chose the other nonentity for a father, it was because that is the way it *should* have been? That Fate has always been misguided, interfering everywhere in her life?

Perhaps the girl will see all this anyway. She will see that Nalia hated the nonentity almost as much as she loved the girl herself. Until now, they have been inseparable, the hating and the loving. Until now, they have ruled her life.

"Ma?" The girl stands in the doorway, golden in the morning light. "Why aren't you practising?"

Nalia waves Maude away. "That's enough now, thank you. Bring me a towel please."

"What happened?" the girl asks. The room smells sour with vomit, stale and sweet and sour. She slumps down onto the dressing table bench, watching Nalia rub herself dry. Did the ghost man see all this? Stomach and breasts, and the flat, high buttocks? A knot fixes itself in her throat — she doesn't know why except that everything is spoilt now. She has spoiled it herself, leading Dirk into every room of the house like a contagion, even into this bathroom. "Ma," she says, "do you want to go for a drive up the coast today?"

"Maybe she should stay in bed," Maude says, setting down a fresh pair of slippers for Nalia, holding her flowered silk gown ready.

"Gugh! If you'd remove that omelette, I'd be fine." Nalia moves gingerly through to the bedroom and opens the windows and the French doors. "What I need is fresh air," she cries.

"Can't you see she's sick?" Maude hisses. "Why you so selfish these days?"

The girl flushes hot under this attack. "What about *you?*" she says. "What about Sonny?"

But Maude just picks up the towel and folds it, smoothing it straight. "Running like a rubbish," she mutters, "bringing rubbish into this house when the madam is gone. Rubbish clothes, rubbish everything." She narrows her eyes at the girl, folded over now, with her face on her knees. Maude's anger has always been an echo of Nalia's own, spiralling up from one sin to the next, and then flaming into fury. When she is like this, it is as if she has no husband — as if she had never taken the girl's hand, and led her through her own house, stood and cried there in front of her. "No use crying," she says now. "What's the use of crying?"

"What's going on in here?" Nalia stands in the doorway, her chin lifted to survey the trouble.

Maude bundles the soiled dressing gown under her arm and is making for the door when the girl looks up and says, "Maude's having a baby."

Maude stiffens and stops. The girl knows that she will never run away from trouble, it is not her way, and immediately, she is sorry. "It's just normal," she mumbles, "She's married now."

"Maude?" Nalia barks. "What's this about?"

"It's just normal," the girl says again, a little louder.

"*Normal?*" cries Nalia, turning on her now. "What do *you* know about normal?"

"Nothing. Thanks to you."

"*What?* Do you *dare* to accuse me? You *snake!* You *traitor!*"

The girl stares up at Nalia, right into her fury. The words are as old as she can remember, and she smiles at the sound of them.

"Maude, is this true?" Nalia holds onto the dressing table, breathing lightly.

But the gate bell rings just then. "There's the dogs," Maude says, making for the door.

"Leave it!" Nalia rasps. She sinks onto the bench, folding herself forward, her arms across her stomach.

"Ma!"

"Madam!" Maude drops the gown and runs. "You want some black tea? Some toast?"

"Just bring me my pills, please. In the drawer next to my bed."

The girl follows Maude into the bedroom. "*Please,*" she says urgently, "please tell me what's wrong with her."

"Knock-knock?" Vi peers around the door. She is waving a telegram. "Natalia there?"

The girl runs over to take it, but Vi snatches it back. "It's for me," she says. "And I want to talk to your mother."

"My mother isn't well." She stares at the telegram, wanting it for herself, longing to have it.

"What is it?" Nalia says, making her way across the room. "A telegram? Bring it here."

Vi shakes her head. "No, my dear. Nothing to do with you this time."

Nalia stares at her, they all stare, even Maude. The simpering is gone. Vi looks around the room, taking her time. "Good news," she says. "I'm going back."

"Ha!" Nalia barks. "The gambler beckons, I suppose?"

"So what if he does, you jealous old hag?" Vi takes a few steps towards Nalia, but the girl blocks her way.

"*What?*" she shouts. "What did you just say to my mother?"

"Leave her," says Nalia. "She's just pathetic. Grotesque."

"Ah!" Vi cries, darting her head around the girl. "The amateur pronounces as usual!"

But the girl suddenly snatches the telegram from her hand. "You *snake!*" she shouts. "You *leech!* You ugly old *hag* yourself! *Get out!* Get out of our house! Maude! Follow her! Don't let her out of your sight until she's through the gate!"

"This is ridiculous!" Vi cries, halfway down the passage. "I am only supposed to leave in two weeks! For God's sake, Maude!"

But Maude pushes behind her, right up to the doorway of her old room. There she stands with her arms folded, while Vi pulls down her suitcase and opens it on the bed.

"Won't you go and tell her?" Vi asks, wheedling again, her mouth hanging open like a baby's.

Maude shakes her head. She has had enough of this woman and her crumbs and her coffee. She's been lucky — Nalia picked her up like that eagle picked up her dog. And now the girl has dropped her again. Well, too bad, hey? The girl needs her mother to herself. She needs her father too. And she needs to remember her own children.

"That's our towel," Maude says, holding out her hand. "That's our Knight's Castile."

So Vi leaves some of her own things behind as well — the leash in the back of the wardrobe, her dirty washing in the basket. She carries her own suitcase downstairs and out to the gate, and only at the last minute does Maude remember the keys.

"Here they are," Vi cries, flinging them into the flowerbed. "Good riddance to bad rubbish!"

Nalia tears up the telegram. "Not the gambler after all," she says.

"What then?" The girl is sitting at her feet with her head on Nalia's lap.

"They want her back for the season." Nalia closes her eyes and rests her head against the back of the chair. She would have rejoiced with Vi after all. When the fight was over, she would have told Maude to bring up a bottle of Veuve Clicquot, and they would have drunk to Vi's good fortune. But the girl does not understand any of this. She has chased Vi off at last, and now it is too late. The girl is all that Nalia has left.

🌸 *10* 🌸

My mother sits in the passenger seat like a stranger, looking around her at the view. I point things out as we make our way up the coast — a monkey with a baby at the side of the road. And then the lagoon, the mangrove swamp with its thick leaves and black, tangled roots.

"I used to be frightened of that swamp," I say. "I thought it was the Hell that Maude was always talking about."

"Ha! Hell is more hellish than that." She rolls down the window, rolls it up again. "I don't feel much like lunch at the hotel today, do you?" she says.

I might have known that she wanted to go to town. She has worn her navy and white piqué, with her peep-toe heels to match.

"Let's have lunch at the Bon Marché," she says, looking at her watch. "Plenty of time to find a parking."

...

Walking down Joubert Street, she puts her arm through mine. Usually, she will take my hand as if I were a child, but now she is leaning on me, suggesting that we stop to see what Cottam's has in the window.

I have seen her perform like this when she is ill — sunk under the eiderdown all afternoon, shivering and hopeless, and then, out before the footlights, brilliant in her magenta silk, closing her eyes as if she is waiting for the coughing in the audience to stop.

"Ma," I say, once we are seated in the Bon Marché, "tell me what's wrong with you."

She frowns down at the menu. Her upper lip is beaded with sweat, so is her forehead. "Toasted cheese and tomato? Anchovy toast? What is it to be?"

If I ask her again, she could slam down her napkin and tell me that I have spoilt her afternoon. So I order and I eat, but all the time I watch her with a dread that sits on my breathing like a stone, ancient and wordless.

She pays the waitress, and then holds on to the table to stand up. All the way to Cottam's, we walk linked together in this strange silence. The noise of the people and the traffic seems to be happening at a great distance. When the street photographer at the pedestrian crossing holds out his card, she doesn't even see me slip it into my pocket. She is staring at a woman standing at the Cottam's lingerie window. "That's one of them!" she says, pointing. "Can you believe it? After all these years?"

The woman turns to look at us. She is tall and stout and she is wearing a hairnet. She is staring at us, as they have all stared over the years — with curiosity, even pity. As soon as she can, she will move off down the street, away from my mother in all her pride and fury.

"Always —" my mother says, pulling on my arm, "*always,* you must be the one who cares the least."

In Cottam's, she settles herself into a chair and lets the saleslady bring things out to us.

"But, Ma," I say, wanting her to remember that I have clothes already, although I don't want to look at them anymore, I don't want to remember them myself.

"Has next year's summer stock come in yet?" she asks.

"No, madam. February, I would think."

"February is too late. What else have you got?"

There is a rush in everything now, as if Naim could arrive at any minute to take me away from her again. When my father caught Dirk glancing his hand across my breast, he smiled. "Dirk the driving teacher!" he cried. "There's my Theadora!"

My mother has pushed her glasses onto her head and is scrutinising the stitching of a seam on a pair of winter slacks. Her face is cool, and her frown, as she holds the slacks up to the light, is what I might have forgotten were I not seeing it again now.

"It's rubbish," she says, handing it back to the saleslady. "Let's go home," she says to me. "We'll have Maude make us some tea before the taxi driver comes to fetch her. Ha!"

Towards the end, they all come on stage, even the ones who have been locked out, despised, hated, ridiculed, and ignored. Nalia has lost her power to keep them away, so she tells Maude to make excuses for her, like Penelope, to keep them downstairs and lock her door. Lying in the gloom of her darkened bedroom, she listens to the rumble of their alien voices below — dark, frightening, unnatural.

"Write this," she whispers to Maude. "'Fathers are nothing. They are an accident of fate.'"

Maude looks up from the notebook in her lap. "Why you causing more trouble now?"

Nalia closes her eyes, panting a little. "Do as you are told!"

So Maude concentrates on curving the letters along the lines of the notebook in her beautiful mission school script. Now that the mother is dying, the girl herself is almost as mad. Every night, she sleeps in Nalia's spare bed, like a husband, and during the day she wears Nalia's clothes, anything she likes. If they are too big, she pins them at the waist with the diamond clips. She wears the best pearls like beads, even in the bath. Nalia has given her everything except the pearl-and-amethyst bracelet and the gold watch, which she has given to Maude. But Sonny can't stand the sight of them and she has had to hide them away. He is jealous of Nalia, he is like a madman himself.

So what is he going to do when the baby comes? Be jealous of that, too? Maude shakes her head. If he tries that, she will take the baby and go to Dorothy. Or she will find a place of her own, just like Nalia.

"Okay," she says. "What must I write now?"

"Write, 'Katzenbogen is your father.'"

"What you saying now?"

Nalia closes her eyes again. She does this to frighten Maude, to shut her up. Anyway, Maude can't help doing as she is told. Now that the Devil of death is here at last, Maude will never desert her.

"I will spell it for you," Nalia says. "Listen carefully please —"

Maude writes one letter at a time. As long as she is up here with Nalia, the girl will go downstairs and talk to her father or to her husband. But never to Katzenbogen. She is jealous of him because he is the only one to whom Nalia will listen now. If Katzenbogen says she must take her medicine, she takes it. If he says she must rest, she even sends the girl away.

"Now read it back to me," Nalia says.

"Why you causing this trouble?"

"I had a dream. Read it back to me."

Maude reaches for her rosary. She keeps it here, away from Sonny. She keeps her statue, too, and her candle, just in case. "The Devil comes in dreams," she says.

The door opens and the girl comes into the room, pale and sallow. "Hello, Ma," she says.

"Will you read to me?" Nalia whispers. "His mother and that photograph?"

The girl stretches out on the spare bed, sorting through her diaries. As soon as Vi left, she brought them in here and read them to Nalia one by one. While she read, it was as if she were writing them for her all over again, as if nothing had changed, and there were still the two of them just as before, a whole future stretching out before them.

Maude slips the notebook behind the cushion of the chair. "I'll bring some tea and your stewed apple," she says to Nalia.

When she is gone, the girl begins to read. Nalia always asks her for the same bits — how he chose her, how he had tears in his eyes. The girl scoffs as she reads, she mocks, as if she had never curled onto the floor outside his study door, or gone to him in his bath — as if even now she does not look at him across the lounge, remembering the smell of his skin, and of his cognac, and of the strange island soap. When Dirk phoned the other day, he had to repeat his name twice. "My husband is here," she said, "He is staying with my father on the launch."

"I know all that," Dirk shouted. "He offered me a job overseas! What kind of rubbish are you people? What does he think I am, hey?"

Nalia has fallen asleep, white as soap on the pillow. She is like a small bird now, with her enormous eyes and her grey hair wild around her head. When Katzenbogen explained to the girl that the pain pills were making Nalia sleepy, she walked away before he could finish his sentence. He is almost as gaunt as her mother, sallow and bony, and she cannot bear him to look at her.

Only when she hears her father and Naim at the front door does she go downstairs now. Or when Katzenbogen himself comes up to see her mother. She has seen him sitting on her mother's bed, talking softly to her in a strange language, smoothing back her hair. And it is again as if she is looking at a life in which she herself is nothing. In which she does not even exist.

She wanders through to Nalia's dressing room to stare into the wardrobe. The clothes are out of order, some have slipped off their hangers. When she tries them on, she knows that she looks ridiculous, but the silk on her skin, the smell of her mother in everything, makes her forget for a moment the horrible sight of the morning sun through the curtains, hot and hopeful, the other life to go back to.

She lifts out the flowered silk dressing gown and throws it over her shoulders like a cloak. Maude is creaking up the back stairs with the tea and stewed apple. She comes and goes up here as if death itself were just another nuisance. And yet every morning the girl waits for the sound of her key in the kitchen door. When she hears it, she slips down the back stairs to sit at the big table in the kitchen and watch Maude tie on her apron. Her stomach is beginning to bulge, and the skin is darkening around her eyes. When Sonny comes to fetch her, he stops the car outside Mrs. Holmes's house, hooting if she is late. "There's the grim reaper," Nalia will say to her. "On your way then."

The girl stands in the dressing room, listening to Maude coaxing Nalia, whispering to her. "Some tea now? Some apple?"

"No."

Maude sighs. "Where must I put this thing then?"

The girl peers in. Maude is holding Nalia's notebook up. "This thing?"

"In the drawer."

"She'll find it there."

"Locked drawer."

"Everyone has keys now."

"Then you keep it. Hide it somewhere in the kitchen. Show it to her when I'm dead."

It is only six o' clock, and already the kitchen is damp with the bread rising for tomorrow, dishcloths soaking in bowls. Every evening, Maude lays out a cold supper for Katzenbogen and the girl on the dining room table, but every evening the girl comes down early to find a bunch of litchis or a banana, and then she takes them upstairs to eat on the verandah. Nalia cannot stand the smell of food anymore, or the noise of a car, or even the roughness of a nightie on her skin. Maude must make her bed with the oldest linen sheets they have, never mind if they are torn. And the girl herself must be careful of how she touches her. She has to keep her voice low, almost at a whisper.

She stands in the kitchen, scanning the hiding places. She has never been able to stand the secrets her mother and Maude keep between them — locking her out, locking her in, doing things for her own good. What was the point of all those secrets in the end? What is the point of them now?

All afternoon, she has waited for Sonny to hoot, and then for the gate to slam. She looks around at the drawers, the cupboards, the top of the fridge. But Maude would be cleverer than that. She would find a place where the servants don't go, where the girl herself would not think of going, either.

Maude has always had her own logic — putting colours together, although Nalia is always telling her that a blue skirt has nothing necessarily to do with a blue blouse. So where would she have put a notebook? Not with the other books in the study — anyone would see it there. She brought it downstairs with the tea things on the tray. The girl opens the cupboard where the tea set is kept. Then she looks into the tray cupboard, pulling the trays out one by one, taking care not to clatter them.

And then, suddenly, there it is — nested into the big silver platter that is never used except when her father comes for dinner. She takes it out and stares at it for a moment. And then she carries it over to the table to read.

🕸 *12* 🕸

Naim's ship is anchored just beyond the bay. He has brought it here to take me back to the island, but he never says this. Until my mother dies, no one talks about the future.

I sit against the pillar to watch the hadedahs swoop and wail across the sky. If I tell Naim that he has married an accident of fate, will he leave me here and give my children to Sonja? Would she send them away, like the blind woman's? Or take them down to the village to be killed and thrown in the sea?

These are the questions I have been asking myself for the weeks since I read my mother's notebook. She herself will not help me. When I told her what I knew, she just closed her eyes. It is as if she has left me already, as if she has been leaving me all along, right from the day that I left her.

Every day, I sit out here on the verandah. Katzenbogen is always with her now. When I listen at the door, I hear her asking him questions, one after another, in their strange language, and then I hear him answer. But if I go in, she just closes her eyes again, and he says nothing.

"Theadora." He is standing in the doorway, with his hands in his pockets. He has never used my name before, so I know what he has come to tell me. But I wait where I am, looking at him. I don't hate him anymore. I can see now that I have his sharp nose and high, broad forehead. And yet he is a stranger to me. He will always be a stranger.

"It is over, Theadora," he says. His voice has the same lilt as my mother's, the same strange dip at the end of my name. "Go to her now."

I climb down off the balustrade and walk past him, up the stairs, along the passage, and into her room. She is there just as before, but her chin is lifted, her eyes are closed as if she were going to sing.

"Ma?" I say, pulling the sheet down. When they are here with her, the sheet must be kept up to her chin. Even Maude won't let me look. But now here she is. Her body is slim as a fish and the lovely roundness of her stomach has vanished into folds of skin, her breasts are flaps. But her legs are still beautiful, smooth and white. "Ma," I say, lying down next to her, folding myself around her. I lay my head on her neck, forgetting completely that she cannot bear to be touched. "Ma," I say, "Oh, Ma! You have beautiful legs!"

"Theadora." Katzenbogen is lifting me away from her. "Let me sit you over here," he says, leading me to her chair.

I watch him draw the sheet back up, right over her head, and then take her mohair blanket and cover the mirror with it. He doesn't look at me, he walks to the French doors and stands there, tearing at his shirt, crying like a baby.

❧ *13* ❧

By the time Naim and my father arrive at the house, my mother is not to be seen. Two women are sitting up there with her body, and they have locked everyone out, even my father. It was Katzenbogen who arranged all this, and now he too has disappeared. His things are gone from Maude's room, and she has found out that I have taken the notebook.

"You going back to that island?" she says, assembling the drinks tray with the best glasses, a dish of olives that my father always likes.

She has asked me this several times, and every time I shrug. But I know now that I will go back with Naim, and that I will keep my mother's lie hidden, as she did herself. One day, I will tell him the truth. But first, I will find a way to bring my children here. I will put the padlock back on the gate, and ask Katzenbogen to return my diaries to me. Until then, I will leave my mother's notebook locked in her drawer, and I will lock up the house as she did. I will ask Maude to drape the furniture and take the dogs to her own house.

"Everyone has troubles," she says. She wears a homemade maternity dress now, and when she hears Sonny hoot, she clicks her tongue. "It's not right that no one can see her," she says, rolling her eyes up towards my mother's room. "Every day, I washed her and put oil on her skin, and now I'm locked out and she's with strangers."

Her rosary is back in her pocket, I can hear it clinking as she moves around the kitchen. "Rock of Ages," she begins, but she can't go on. Suddenly, she stands quite still, in the middle of the kitchen and lifts her apron to her face. "It's terrible," she cries, "I've lost her now and it's terrible for me too."

Naim leads me out onto the verandah, right over to the balustrade. The sun is bright on the bay, lighting his ship out there. "We will go home on her again," he says gently. "But by a different route this time. All right?"

I have already packed the two street photographs of my mother and me into the suitcase. I will put them side by side, with her bottle of Madame Rochas between them. When she asked me to give my diaries to Katzenbogen, I did. And then, downstairs, when he tried to give them back, I wouldn't take them. What are they anyway without her to hear them? Without her to listen? What am I myself, now that I am no longer a daughter?

In a month I will be turning twenty, and I think I understand the sadness of life. If my mother had been able to listen, I would have told her this. I would have told her more, too — things that I have seen for myself, that I have known for myself as well.

"Here," says my father, handing me a glass of whiskey. "Drink this down."

He goes to stand at the other end of the verandah, staring out, saying nothing. I know that he is furious with death the way he is furious with everything that gets in his way. I know now, too, that he loved my mother, and that he loves her still. He loved her just as she loved him — two furious people who always kept me between them.